FOOLISH

THINGS

A Southern Tale

By William Blaylock

Flat Toad Road Conceptions
55842 CR 430
Winona, Mississippi 38967

willblaylock61@icloud.com

To the memory of my loving father who's healthy balance of humor and earnest taught me to be responsible while having fun along the way.

And to the loving memory of my sister Vicki. She was my first playmate, who shared with me a commonality greater than either of us ever knew.

Acknowledgments

The writing of this book has been a labor of love. The hours spent in prayer seeking God's help has brought me closer to him. Although the stories are not true, they caused me to reminisce about my family who I love dearly. I want to thank God for the journey and thank my family for the memories that sparked an imagination. Also to my wife, Sherry, who allowed me the solitary time away from her to write. Thanks to Dr. Finis Beauchamp, my proofreader, who carved time out of his tight schedule to do me a favor. And finally, I thank my friends and family who were willing to read through rough drafts as they materialized. That would be Katherine Peggy Land, Tara Bargonah, Janie Webb, Jimmy Gant, Winnie Blaylock and my dear wife Sherry. They offered encouragement and the constructive criticism I needed to form this into a sweet southern tale.

Prologue

All of the many fern covered hollows and creeks
that served as a playground when I was a child
have merged in my imagination to create one
magnificent place. That wonderful place has become the back drop to this story and is painted
clearly in my mind by fond memories collected
through the years.

At first glance, the reader will suppose that this
story is taking place sometime within the 19th
century. However, it becomes apparent as the
story unfolds that the rural Mississippi culture
represented was indeed tucked away in time.
The cause of their antiquation, even after the in-
vention of modern technology, was due to the
absence of electricity. This deficit caused a sep-
aration between them and metropolitan cultures,
even later than the timeline of this novel which is
set in the 1940's and 50's.

Chapter 1

Lizzie Pickle walked cautiously down the worn path, holding her dress with both hands as she cradled the bail of a rusty water bucket in the crease of her right elbow.

Lizzie was in the last days of her last month of pregnancy. She strained her delicate neck to look past the bucket on one side and her navel, which protruded like the left knee of a bullfrog, on the other. After meticulous effort, Lizzie made it to the bottom of the slippery bank and stood before the aqua tinted spring. She was mesmerized by the beautiful blue water as she thought about the baby she was carrying and the warning she received from Miss Rhody who was the closest thing to a mother that she could remember. She was also her closest neighbor and the community midwife. Miss Rhody knew everything there was to know about carrying and birthing babies even though she never carried one of her own. Lizzie had already been scolded by Miss Rhody the previous week when she caught her coming up the hill with a full bucket of water. She demanded that Lizzie carry only a half bucket of water on each trip to the spring. It meant more walking, but walking was good for her.

The Artesian spring bubbling from the volcanic aquifer deep below the hillside, produced water for her family and many others living along the ridges above the beautiful, misty hollow which had become the namesake of their community.

Lizzie's husband, Albert, built a bottomless square cypress box into the ground which caressed the spring, causing it to pool and spill over into the rocky creek. The small creek grew as other spring heads along the floor of the hollow made continuous contributions, while on it's meandering trek through the dark forest. Albert nostalgically referred to the forest as, *The Hardwoods,* because his grandfather always called them by that name.

Leaf-covered hills towered above the creek like two strong shoulders placed there by some unseen hand. The tall hills followed the creek for a distance of one mile, where they abruptly ended as two steep bluffs, and stood as a gateway into the enchanted narrow gorge.

A mist arose from the cold spring water as it collided with the sweltering heat of the Mississippi climate. The brisk cool water bubbled and splashed over rocks, sprinkling the banks, causing the ferns and buckeyes to flourish, creating a lush green hollow that beckoned wanderers to experience the peace and tranquillity found there.

As Lizzie stood near the spring, she looked into the pleasant hollow. The creek, filled with sandstones and pebbles, offered its invitation to come; so, she went. She set her bucket beside the spring and traipsed along the ancient path following the creek.

Pudgy dark green moss covered the shady banks and rocks like a soft quilt. The tender leaves of beech trees along the hillsides were beginning to break forth from their buds. The ferns uncurled as if yawning and stretching from a long winter's sleep. An outcropping of very large sandstones lay along the ridge in a pile like a giant had discarded them from his field. Dogwoods, in full bloom, dotted the woods' edge.

The path turned slightly from the moss covered bank and then descended into the creek. Lizzie hopped from stone to stone, finding her way to the middle of the creek. She finally landed on a large stone where she remained for a moment imagining all the people, both past and present, who had stood where she now stands: first, the Choctaws, then, Albert's distant grandfather, Atticus Payne, who braved unimaginable perils before settling this hollow for his family, and now her family. Perhaps there were even people before the Choctaws who roamed these woods.

She picked up a long stick leaning against the bank and tested it for strength. "Seemed sturdy enough" she thought, as she hooked it underneath a sandstone the size of a skillet. Flipping the rock over caused a scurry of salamanders as they sought refuge from the daylight.

Lizzie's attention was diverted from the salamanders when a rumbling of thunder shook the ground causing her to glance upward through the thick canopy of trees. The ominous, black cloud rolled and angrily swallowed the clear sky before it. Leaves fluttered across her face as they were tossed up from the ground like a garden salad. Giant oak trees rocked back and forth against each other like drunk men. Debris fell from the sky.

Fear gripped her heart as she thought about Charlie, her four year old son, whom she had left sleeping peacefully on her momma's quilt. It was common practice to get water from the spring before Charlie missed her and she hoped this time would be no different.

Her concern was also for Miss Rhody, whom she loved like a mother. The year was 1942. Eight months earlier, Albert was drafted into the army. He had asked Stanley and Miss Rhody Fletcher to look after his family until his return. Little did he know that one month after his departure, Stanley would be killed when a load of logs rolled off of a wagon and crushed him. Miss Rhody was devastated by his death. She still grieved her mother's passing from the previous year; not to mention, the murder of her father in prison. It seemed as though Miss Rhody was plagued by heartache and loss.

It was Stanley's endearment and kind affection that made him give her the nickname "Miss Rhody". The nickname caught on and everyone else began to call her that too.

Her father was a violent and loveless man. Her brother Roy, who had left home as a young man, was distant and complacent about everyone else's needs but his own. He only came home to take possession of the family farm when their mother died. Stanley was the one good thing in her life and now he was gone.

It was Stanley's endearment and kind affection that made him give her the nickname "Miss Rhody". The nickname caught on and everyone else began to call her that too.

It was Stanley who introduced Albert to Lizzie. He even let them borrow his truck for their first date. Of course, he was the chaperone. Stanley dragged Miss Rhody's arm chair and hassock out of the house and loaded it into the back of the truck. What a sight! Albert driving down the road as Stanley reclined in Miss Rhody's armchair with his feet propped up on the hassock. His was the most coveted seat at the drive in theater! Of course, Miss Rhody demanded that he clean all the popcorn from under the cushion before he was allowed to bring it back into the house! Albert and Lizzie laughed often about their first date with Stanley!

Lizzie and Charlie moved in with Miss Rhody for a while after the accident so she would be surrounded by people who loved her, as she mourned for Stanley and attempted to make sense of his business affairs.

Besides being Stanley's wife, she was also his secretary, and had been for their entire marriage. She knew every detail of the business except the intricacies of actually running it, so she reluctantly sold it to their competitor.

The grief of losing Stanley was compounded when she was forced to sell the business, which had not only made their living, but was well established before Rhody met Stanley. It was a part of him and now they were both gone, leaving only the memories and the guilt of not being able to hold on to something that Stanley loved so much.

Lizzie's gratitude towards Miss Rhody was immense considering all the help she was to her as a young and confused little girl. Everything Lizzie knew about life was taught to her by Miss Rhody, who practiced healthy virtues along with practicality. She possessed a strong faith in God and claimed to be personally acquainted with Him. Although Lizzie loved and held the greatest respect for her, she doubted that anyone could know God personally.

When she and Albert lost their infant daughter, Marie, to pneumonia, Miss Rhody comforted them with her gentle compassion and lovely words from the Bible. She always said, "Jesus is the Word," and "The words I speak from the Bible are alive." Statements like that made no sense to Lizzie, but there was no denying that the words possessed a strange medicinal power that somehow brought comfort for their grieving souls.

Stanley Fletcher met Lizzie's father, Rosamond Stuckey, on a logging job in Eutaw, Alabama. While there, he asked Rosamond if he would be interested in managing his sawmill in Misty Hollow. Because Lizzie's family had fallen on hard times due to the recent deaths of her mother and newborn brother, Rosamond accepted the offer. That's how Lizzie acquired her surrogate mother, Miss Rhody.

As Lizzie recalled past experiences of family and friends, the thoughts held full sway of her present awareness. It wasn't until another clap of thunder rumbled and shook the ground that her focus was restored to the danger surrounding her and she prayed, "God, if you can hear me, save Charlie, save Miss Rhody, and save my baby!"

In eagerness to get home to Charlie, Lizzie ran along the ancient path through the swirling leaves. Just as she could see the open field beyond *The Hardwoods'* edge, a dead limb the size of a man's arm fell from overhead and struck her like a club across her shoulders. Dazed and thrown to the ground, Lizzie lay there groaning. Her head swam and the roar of the howling storm faded in and out as she fell out of consciousness and back in again. The rain pelting her face began as large drops, but quickly escalated into tiny whips, as the howling wind forced the raindrops from the sky like a barrage of arrows.

Determined to save her boy, she rolled over onto her knees and began to crawl. Hail, the size of dimes, stung through her thin cotton dress and bounced on the ground like marbles.

The storm intensified and trees began to crash down from the ridges above her head. She reached for a grape vine that draped over several large boulders. By weakened arms and legs, she pulled herself up, noticing a natural shelter under the large stones.

Suddenly, immense pain stabbed her womb like a sharp knife in the gut.

"No!" She thought, "Not now!"

Falling to her knees, Lizzie reluctantly crawled inside the small rock shelter. She had barely made refuge inside the opening when a barricade in the form of a tree top fell from the sky blocking the entrance to the small cave. Lizzie turned to face strong oak limbs that held her captive like the bars of a jail. She pulled and tugged at the branches hoping to escape, but they were immovable. She was trapped!

Feverishly, she dug with her bare hands only to hit a rock bottom. While kneeling, the sensation of warm water ran down her legs filling the craters where her knees were imbedded in the soft sand. Her water had broken! The baby was coming!

Lizzie thought about her previous deliveries: Charlie was the first and the most difficult. Then the miscarriage which changed her forever. Not long afterwards, Marie was conceived. What a perfect angel she was....

It saddened Lizzie when she thought about the day Marie died and how impossible it was to save her from the pneumonia that took her. And now, here she was in this predicament. Her un-delivered baby in danger and Charlie could be blown away by the storm. She felt helpless, as if she were about to lose her whole family. She knew that this baby was coming, with or without help! She only hoped the baby wasn't breached.

Perhaps God would help. She was raised to believe in God. Her daddy had strong faith, but hers was always a little anemic. She never could make the connection to a personal God. To her, He was just out there somewhere, maybe, a gray bearded old man sitting on a throne, sternly looking down on all the people and waiting for the opportunity to punish them for breaking His rules.

Something her father said many times came to her thoughts, "God would never leave us; nor forsake us." She didn't know if this promise was true or not, but if it was, she needed it now and hoped that God would somehow fix this mess. She was sure that it was normal for some people, in some backwards places in the world, to birth their babies in caves, but not in Mississippi.

There was no need to scream for help because there was none to be had. No one would be able to hear her in this deep hollow, under this big rock. Lizzie sat down, then fell gently back on the cold sand hoping to relieve the severity of the pain. She raised her pelvis to remove the cotton knickers she had made herself, out of decorative flour sacks.

The contractions were getting more severe and coming at five minute intervals. There was a strong urge to push. Lying against the rock wall, with cupped hands, she embraced her thighs while peering between her legs. Recalling Miss Rhody's previous instructions, she began to pant. Lizzie was careful to breath and push at the correct times as the baby came forward naturally. Very shortly, she could see her baby. There was something else too! The umbilical cord stretched tight across the crown of the baby's head! She reached for the cord and ran her finger underneath it, gently releasing the fetus. Suddenly there was another strong contraction. Lizzie screamed with pain. She cupped her hands under her thighs again and pushed and cried. Soon, another strong contraction. Lizzie screamed again. She pushed and screamed. The baby was coming slowly as Lizzie pushed and screamed one last time. The final push launched the baby from its chrysalis into the wet sand.

Through tear soaked eyes, Lizzie endearingly drew the baby to her bosom. Born with a full head of black hair, it was a girl. She seemed healthy in every way. But she was not breathing! Lizzie grasped her newborn by the ankles like she had seen Miss Rhody do and gave her a stinging slap across her bottom. The baby's squeal sounded like music to her ears. What a beautiful sound.

Lizzie's crying was reduced to a whimper as she comforted the squalling newborn. Suddenly, there was movement outside the shelter! Lizzie ceased her whimpering momentarily in an effort to listen.

Charlie's little voice came yelling into the cave,

"Momma? You in there? Why are you crying?" He stood on the other side of the fallen tree. His chin was resting on top of his two little, limb clutched hands with his bright blue eyes peering into the cave.

"Momma, come out! Who is that with you?" Lizzie responded, "We're trapped Buddy! We can't get out!"

Buddy was Charlie's nickname. Lizzie nostalgically gave him that name after her father, who was called "Buddy" by all the people around Eutaw.

Miss Rhody came stumbling through the debris, finally catching up to Charlie and peering into the cave. Lizzie whispered to herself, "Thank God she came!"

Earlier Miss Rhody stood on her porch watching the menacing dark cloud as it swelled to cover the entire sky. She became frightened when suddenly, a long tail dropped from the cloud like a twisting spiral and touched the ground. Her heart pounded in her chest as if it would escape and flee from her body. The spiraling pillar quickly transformed into a large funnel, spinning and slinging its tail like a bullwhip, striking the ground and casting trees through the air in an effortless manor as though they were blades of grass.

She watched in horror as the tornado thrashed about, destroying the tops of *The Hardwoods* above the hollow, then across the garden behind Lizzie's house. It looked as if

Lizzie's house was about to be destroyed. But Miss Rhody prayed, "Lord place your mighty hand of protection over Lizzie and Charlie!"

The tornado immediately changed direction and traveled the length of the high pasture away from Lizzie's house. Miss Rhody pulled her dress above her knees, sprang off of her porch, and ran up the road. She reached the front porch of Lizzie's cabin just as the tornado re-treated, withdrawing its tail back up into the black clouds overhead. Wheezingly, she yelled from the steps, "Lizzie?" There was no answer. Alarmed by the silence, Miss Rhody stepped onto the porch and approached the door. She reached for the door knob as Charlie opened the door rubbing his little eyes and yawning.

"Hey Miss Rhody! What you doing?" He had been sleeping, untouched by the storm.

Not wanting to alarm Charlie, she noncha-lantly asked, "Where's your momma?" Then she noticed that Lizzie's water bucket was gone and she thought, "God help her! She's at the Spring!"

She clasped Charlie's hand and with gentle determination said, "Let's go find your momma." He led her like a dog on a leash down into the hollow and then released himself from her grip. He noticed the fallen trees accompanied by the sound of a crying baby. He curiously followed the sound through the mass of fallen trees up to the front of the rock shelter. Miss Rhody rushed to the cave entrance where Charlie stood. Peeping through the fallen treetop, she shouted, "Are you alright Lizzie? Is your Baby ok?"

To quiet the screaming, Lizzie brought the baby to her bosom, while replying, "We're al-right. Can you help us out of here!?" Relieved to hear Lizzie's voice, Miss Rhody looked through the limbs at the sucking baby.

"You sure did bring a pretty one into the world! Don't you worry! Me and Charlie will have ya'll out of there in two shakes of a stick!"

Sizing up the situation, Miss Rhody decided that the old buck saw hanging on the wall of Lizzie's porch would cut those limbs with ease. "Charlie stay here with your momma and sister while I get the saw!" Charlie responded, "Yes Ma'am."

Miss Rhody removed enough limbs to gain access into the tight space beside Lizzie and her newborn. Charlie followed close behind leaning onto her back in an effort to see his momma and the new, little, crying stranger.

She brought a small blanket to swaddle the baby. But Lizzie had used her knickers as a makeshift swaddle. The baby was stuffed into one leg of the home made knickers, like pota- toes in a sack. The drawstring was tied, in a loose bow, around the baby's neck and the oth- er leg wrapped around the newborn like a blan- ket. The umbilical cord streamed out of the top along with the baby's head.

Miss Rhody laughed when she saw the con- traption; however, she was also relieved to see that the baby was warm. She cut the umbilical cord with a straight razor that she kept in her pocket. As a midwife, she was always prepared for an emergency.

While helping Lizzie to withdraw backwards from under the shelter, she continued to comfort and reassure her,

"Now don't you worry about anything. I'll heat some water and clean ya'll up when we get home."

Lizzie was relieved to have Miss Rhody's help. It looked like everything was going to be okay. Her baby was well and Charlie was untouched by the storm. Lizzie mumbled a prayer to her impersonal god, "Thank you, God for sending my momma and for saving my family!"

Chapter 2

A subtle, but unsettling darkness loomed over Lizzie's soul. She sat in the porch swing, lethargically holding her two month old sleeping baby, while Charlie napped in the breezeway on his grandmother's old quilt.

Lizzie's melancholy thoughts drifted to her husband and she spoke negatively to herself, "His family is growing and he is somewhere in Europe fighting with a bunch of strangers!" Then she felt guilt for her negative comment and began to contemplate, "What if he didn't make it home? How could I go on without him? How would I take care of our children?" The idea of him not coming home rattled her emotions. The weighty darkness intensified suppressing any feeling of hope.

Despair fully engulfed her soul. The once radiant glow of pregnancy faded from her beautiful face. Covert malevolence, of every good thing, began to harbor inside her heart. In a desperate effort to regain her mental stability, she focused her thoughts on positive things. Once again, she spoke to herself, "It is a gorgeous spring day. The birds are singing. We are all safe from the tornado. Our house didn't get blown away. And look, here comes Miss Rhody bringing the mail!"

Miss Rhody happily bounced up onto the porch, but immediately she noticed the expression on Lizzie's face. It was the same expression she had seen many times before. She first saw it on her momma's face when she was a little girl, growing up in an abusive home. She'd seen it at other times on the women she helped after the birthing of their babies. Miss Rhody feared for Lizzie because she knew from experience that these things can turn very ugly. The women who suffer from this sometimes lose their way.

She once had a patient in Salters Flat, who drowned her three children in the same wash pot in which she washed their clothes. Her husband came home to find the children dead around the wash pot, while his wife was hanging clothes on the line, humming to herself seemingly unaware of what she had done.

Miss Rhody cautiously opened conversation, "How are you feeling today Lizzie? Is the little girl sleeping and eating okay?" Lizzie bluntly answered, "I'm fine—just very tired—a little depressed — I'm trying to think happy thoughts — It sure is a beautiful day....The baby stays up all night—sleeps all day—I've got to get her on schedule somehow."

Miss Rhody spoke reassuringly, "I'll come stay with you and help with the baby. Since Albert is away, you need help— Oh yea, I almost forgot! You have a letter from Albert!"

Lizzie lethargically received the letter as Miss Rhody opened and placed it in her free hand. She produced an almost listless smile as she began to read the letter. The faint smile gradually faded and was replaced by a stone face.

The open letter fell from her limp hand onto the floor. At the same time, she unlocked her elbow and allowed the sleeping baby to slide into her lap unattended. Miss Rhody quickly, but gently removed the baby from Lizzie's lap while exclaiming, "Oh my dear! What has happened!?" There was no response, only a dead, blank stare. Miss Rhody bent to retrieve the letter just as Charlie woke from his nap. He waddled over to his brazen faced mother, leaning against her leg expecting the usual loving affection, but instead, she exploded with rage. She pushed him to the floor and indignantly screamed, "Get away from me! I don't want you!" Charlie cried as he ran off of the porch down into *The Hardwoods.*

Miss Rhody lovingly glared at Lizzie as Charlie disappeared into the woods. She shook the letter open with her one free hand to read what it said:

Dearest Lizzie,
Words cannot begin to express how much I love and miss you and Charlie. I am unable to write a long letter due to time constraints. I only write this letter to inform you that your cousin Eddy was killed by anti-tank artillery. He died a hero, just as the thousands of others who are giving their lives to liberate the world.
If I do not make it out alive, please know that you and Charlie have meant everything to me. Nothing else in this world matters to me except your love and welfare. I may never see our new baby. For that, I have the deepest regret. But my life insurance should support you and the children for a long time, until you are able to get your bearings. Please remember me fondly and hug the children for me.

Your loving
affectionate husband,
Albert

Miss Rhody folded the letter while attempting to hold back the tears. It was obvious by Albert's letter that the fighting was intense. Also, he didn't expect to make it out alive and was saying good bye to his family. She didn't want to make things worse by displaying her emotions in front of Lizzie. She carried the sleeping baby into the bedroom and placed her in the crib. After weeping softly for a few moments, she collected herself and then returned to Lizzie hoping to comfort and settle her. She didn't know how she was going to retrieve Charlie from the woods and watch Lizzie and the baby all at once. None of them could be left alone for any period of time. Lizzie needed sleep, but she was almost unapproachable in her current frame of mind. Miss Rhody cautiously reached for Lizzie's hand and beckoned her to leave the porch swing. Surprisingly, there was no negative reaction as she obediently followed her into the house. After putting Lizzie to bed, she hoped the baby did not wake and that Charlie would come home when he finished licking his wounds.

Miss Rhody went into the kitchen and cooked a big supper. The smell of home cooking drew Charlie out of hiding. He came slinking up onto the porch hoping to stay out of his angry mother's sight. Miss Rhody's open arms were waiting for him. He fell into her embrace and cried until her dress was wet with tears.

"Why is momma mad at me?" Miss Rhody gently whispered, "She's not mad honey. She is only tired. We need to let her rest and give her some space, until she recovers from birthing the baby."

Three weeks later, the darkness slowly retreated and Lizzie's heart began to find hope again. Miss Rhody had been there night and day caring for her and the children. The baby was on schedule and she was sleeping most of the night. During all of that time, Lizzie sat in the porch swing each day staring into space, lost in her invisible prison of depression. Miss Rhody hand fed her when she would eat, bathed her as often as she could, and put her to bed every night.

Lizzie saw Charlie peeking at her around the gardenia bush near the porch where she sat. She smiled and silently beckoned for him to come to her. Charlie was apprehensive, but he slowly crept up to her. She hugged him, expressing the kind of love that only a mother can give and then softly asked him for his forgiveness. Charlie squeezed her tight in conciliation and then tighter as if she might slip out of his embrace. He remained there in the comfort of his mother's arms and then said, "I love you momma."

It was good not only to know, but to feel the deep love and forgiveness of her son. Especially after her mean spirited rejection of him. The chemical imbalance of postpartum had triggered the despair and callousness that held reign over her emotions and clouded her mind. Charlie released her from his endearing hug and descended the front steps just as Miss Rhody came from inside the house with the fretting baby. She saw the smile on Lizzie's face and knew that the storm was finally over.

She asked, "Are you feeling well enough to nurse this sweet little girl?" Without a word, Lizzie gladly reached for her baby and lifted the bundle immediately to her bosom. The baby grunted while gulping her momma's abundant reserve of warm milk.

Lizzie looked down at her bundle endearingly as she nursed. That pleased Miss Rhody, but she decided to test the waters to make certain that Lizzie's emotions were actually under control.

She mentioned, "Albert wrote another letter two weeks ago— Since you weren't able, I read it— He said that he was sorry to send you such a dire report, but at the time, he truly thought he would not make it out alive. He is safe now and on leave....He also said your Uncle Ed has requested that Eddie's body be shipped back to Eutaw, Alabama for burial, but the war department informed him that Eddie was already buried in a military cemetery near the battlefield."

Miss Rhody could literally see the glow come back into Lizzie's face as the fear and uncertainty of Albert's survival subsided. Although the news concerning cousin Eddy held its own place of sadness in her heart, the good news of her husband's safety released her bottled up emotions and she cried tears of relief.

Lizzie exclaimed, "Oh God, thank you! I was so worried! I've been sitting here wondering if I might be a widow, but I was afraid to ask!"

They both sat silent for a moment, meditating on the news. Then Lizzie perplexingly said, "It is so sad that Eddie is buried in Europe away from all family. I wish he had been buried next to daddy in Eutaw."

Lizzie thought about the last time she saw her father, Rosemond Stuckey, walking up the muddy road carrying his little suitcase in one hand and a walking stick in the other. Rheumatism left a permanent slump in his back. On the day he left, he was still recovering from a wagon accident that occurred the day before as he helped Albert pull corn.

Uncle Ed was her father's little brother and he pleaded with him to visit them in Eutaw Alabama, where he and Aunt Earline lived. The next week, she received word that her father passed away; and it was decided that he would be buried there, since it was his home. Lizzie and Albert were unable to attend the funeral, due to Marie's frailty; but, at least her poor father was surrounded by other loved ones, especially her three younger brothers, who now lived in Eutaw.

Lizzie reflected on the trouble and difficulties of the past few months. The stress of Albert's absence, the tornado, giving birth, and the depression that would have destroyed them all, if not for Miss Rhody. Due to all of that, the baby was still nameless. Albert and Lizzie corresponded back and forth throughout her pregnancy seeking to settle on a name, but never came to a conclusion.

If it was a boy, Albert wanted to name him Albert Jr., but if it was a girl, he wanted to name her Marie after their first daughter. Lizzie liked both of those names too, but wanted to honor her mother by naming the baby after her. She realized that her mother's name, Enna, attached to the name 'Pickle,' might cause a good bit of consternation. However, it still seemed like the most obvious choice because the name described the conditions surrounding her, since the day she was conceived: her father was drafted right away, her surrogate grandfather, Stanley Fletcher, was killed in an horrific accident, and she was born in the middle of a dangerous tornado, where she was trapped under a giant rock. All those things would most definitely describe her introduction into the world as being "In a pickle!"

Lizzie spoke the name audibly for the first time to see how it sounded, "Enna Pickle....Enna Marie Pickle....yes....that will be her name."

Chapter 3

It was late autumn and the brisk wind caused the multi-colored leaves to fall in mass, leaving the trees nearly naked in *The Hardwoods* below Lizzie's house. The creek at the bottom of the hollow was almost visible from the window closest to her secretary where she sat. This was Albert's and her favorite time of the year and she was lonesome without her husband.

Lizzie turned her attention away from the window and wistfully stuffed a newly written letter into an envelope. She thought about how her letters had become more heartfelt than ever, since Eddie's death and the uncertainty of Albert's survival. His absence caused her tremendous anxiety, but she hoped he did not sense it from their correspondence. She didn't want him to be concerned about the welfare of his family. There was enough for him to worry about just staying alive.

Albert's Uncle Thomas and Aunt Emily owned the only radio in Misty Hollow and they offered Lizzie and the kids a standing invitation to join them for the news concerning the war. The newscaster always began his report with the number of American casualties for each day. That was something Lizzie did not want to hear because of the anonymity of the figure. All of those casualties represented real people with families back home in the states. Like cousin Eddy, his only identification was an impersonal tally mark; a number, as if his life was irrelevant.

Albert was drafted months before the United States entered the war. Since he had completed basic training, he was one of the first soldiers sent into battle. The war seemed endless, or at least it appeared that way. Albert had been gone for much of their short marriage. He was almost a stranger to her and he definitely was a stranger to Charlie and Enna. Lizzie did not blame him for his absence; she only wanted him back home and alive. She certainly was proud of her husband for willingly serving his country in the face of death. Without that kind of sacrifice, their children may not have a future. She deduced in her own mind, as a result of all the history she had ever read, that for the good of the whole world, men must die to protect it from the evil that seeks to destroy it.

Of course, she felt sorry for cousin Eddy; but at the same time, she also selfishly hoped Albert would not be one of those who gave the ultimate sacrifice. She understood the object of war was to kill, or be killed; and it was a miracle anytime a soldier made it out alive. However, knowing the details was depressing, and because of her bout with depression, she never accepted another invitation from Uncle Thomas and Aunt Emily. People say, "Ignorance is bliss." That certainly is a true statement.

Lizzie's serious thought processes began to fade away as she recalled the light hearted contents of the letter she had just written to Albert:

Dear Albert,
Since we could come to no certain agreement on our baby's name, I have taken it on myself to name her after my mother, "Enna," and our angel daughter, "Marie." I'm sure you will get a kick out of that when you realize that your daughter's name sounds like, 'In a pickle' Ha! Ha!
Everyone is well. I love you and miss you very much. Charlie is growing up fast and can't wait for his daddy to come home and buy him a horse! He wants to be a cowboy! The wooden horse that you carved, is his favorite toy. Now, he wants you to carve him a cow so he can rope it! Ha! Ha!"
Also, you should get a laugh out of this too! As I mentioned before, Charlie is growing up fast. Last week, he insisted that he was old enough to go exploring in *The Hardwoods* by himself. It

was a cool and breezy day, so I wrapped him in several layers of clothes. His backpack was loaded with the necessary supplies for a long trip, which included: leftover cold biscuits and bacon from breakfast, and a small bedroll. A butter knife and homemade scabbard were tied around his waist so he would have protection against the bears and wolves, should any come after him. Ha! Ha! He kissed me goodbye and set out on his journey. I watched him from the kitchen window, as he took his hiking stick in hand and descended into *The Hardwoods.*

He stopped and looked at every anomaly along the way, poking at them with his butter knife. Finally, he disappeared into the deep gulley below the house and remained out of sight for a long time. I was about to go check on him, when he suddenly reappeared with a frantic look on his face. He was running as fast as he could, while flailing and swatting at something that was invisible from my perspective at the window. I ran out onto the porch and screamed, "What's wrong Charlie?" He was so occupied with swatting that he didn't answer me. He just stripped off the backpack and flung it, as he ran up the steps and flew into the house. I saw the problem immediately. There were yellow-jackets

swarming around him like he was a slice of wa-
termelon in late summer! Ha! Ha!

When he ran into the house, he brought the yellow-jackets with him. I swatted yellow-jackets
until I was out of breath! Meanwhile, Charlie was
stripping out of his clothes and with every layer
he stripped off, it brought a whole new batch of
yellow-jackets. Finally, Charlie was stripped
down to his underwear and running around the
house still flailing as the yellow-jackets were like
dive bombers coming at both of us. We were
each stung only three times apiece, which was a
miracle, since I killed stray yellow-jackets for two
hours afterwards!

Charlie explained that he saw a hole in the
ground and when he poked his knife into the
hole, the yellow-jackets poured out and chased
him all the way to the house! Anyway, that is all
for now.

We love and miss you,

Lizzie

The postal service did not make deliveries to
her house due to the impassable condition of
the road. All deliveries were made at the cross-

road, which was cluttered with mailboxes; each one standing on its own post; each one representing a household along the south ridge above Misty Hollow.

Throughout each day, Lizzie waved and spoke to the passersby as they trekked through the mud to get their mail: some walking, some on horse or mule, some in wagons, and a few in trucks. But, they all traveled in the same deep ruts in the middle of the road.

With letter in hand, Lizzie walked the short distance to the crossing, where she expected to catch the postman for the purchase of a three cent stamp; and where she also hoped to receive a letter from Albert.

She left Charlie in charge of Enna who was fast asleep in her cradle. Charlie was a considerate boy and played quietly on the floor, being careful not to wake his sister. His toys consisted of one wooden horse, four empty thread spools, cotton string from a flour sack, and a few blocks of wood cut from the end of boards that Albert used to make Charlie's cradle, in which Enna was sleeping.

Charlie stacked the blocks in a circle to create a fence to hold his horse. The spools were cows. And each of the spools had a piece of string tied to them; where, from his imagination, he roped them from his wooden horse. Charlie didn't require someone to occupy him. He played by himself for hours on end, fixated on his own imaginary world.

The postman came and went. There was no letter from Albert, which was not unusual. She knew Albert was not able to write often, but she wrote him weekly anyway, hoping that he got her letters and was encouraged by them.

She returned from the crossroads and settled into the porch swing, just as a gentle rain began to fall. Lizzie loved the therapeutic sound of the drops striking the tin top. The rain water poured from the eve and flooded in all directions away from the house. Watching the rain brought memories of Albert and a story he told her about the ridge on which their house sat.

He called it a "Dividing Ridge." Apparently all of the water that fell onto the south side of the roof drained into the Big Black River, which flows all the way to Grand Gulf, where it enters into the Mississippi River. On the other hand, the water that fell on the north side of the roof drained into the Yazoo River, which meanders past the cotton docks of Greenwood, and eventually flows past the courthouse at Vicksburg, where it enters the Mississippi River.

Even though the water left the ridge going in opposite directions, both tributaries ran into the Mississippi River in the proximity of Vicksburg. The Big Black flows through the hilly side of the state, while the Yazoo flows through the fertile Mississippi Delta.

Besides being full of interesting stories, Albert was also a loving husband and father who provided for his family. She was thankful that he sent most of his salary home every month, except for a mandatory life insurance premium and $1.50 for laundry service, that the Army deducted. Sometimes he kept a couple of dollars for emergency money, but he didn't need much; he had no bad habits.

Lizzie managed to save most of the money Albert sent home because they owed no debts and their expenses were low. She learned frugality from her father, who learned it from his father. Frugality was a trait handed down since the pioneer days and continued out of necessity through all of the hard times of war, reconstruction, and economic depression. Lizzie remembered the oversized gardens that overstocked their pantries with home canned vegetables. There never was a shortage of food. Even the root cellars were full of potatoes, turnips, carrots, beets, and onions which had to be scooped out every year to make room for fresh root crops. Those people knew about hunger and never forgot how it felt. Fear and frugality, along with a healthy dose of folkways, distributed among ensuing generations were valuable traits to possess. It usually meant food in your belly.

Even in Lizzie's day, there was no electricity to enjoy the modern conveniences of which townsfolk had already become accustomed. The people continued to live using old ways and techniques, much like in the 1800s. If not for an occasional automobile or tractor, it would be difficult to tell the difference.

Most of their farming implements were durable mule pulled iron planters and plows already used by several generations before them. The red clay dirt used to raise crops to feed their children was the same red clay dirt that fed their grandparents.

They did not have refrigeration or indoor plumbing. Mules and wagons were still very common. Some people had no transportation. When supplies were needed at home, they hitched a ride to town by hopping on the back of anything rolling down the road. If no transportation came by, they walked the whole distance.

Short cuts were taken on foot paths that led from homestead to homestead throughout the woods. There were few roads, but there was a maze of foot paths.

People pulled together at hog killing time and helped their neighbors. The meat was shared and there was always two fires built in the yard; one to cook the lard from the cracklings and the other for a pot of chitterlin' to be served at supper time when the work was done. Those occasions were bonding times where many children met their future spouses.

Homes were heated with firewood, although propane was becoming popular. Many still cooked on wood stoves. Uncle Thomas bought Aunt Emily a gas stove to save himself from the back breaking work of cutting stove wood, but she refused to cook on it. She said, "It just didn't cook the food right."

Some people owned iceboxes. But, most were like Lizzie and buried a block of ice in a bed of sawdust in the ground. The saw dust was adequate insulation and preserved the ice until the truck came by on its weekly route.

Uncle Thomas and Aunt Emily had the only telephone in the community, after several local men cut and installed black locust poles from town to Misty Hollow. Uncle Thomas paid the monthly telephone bill, but everyone who helped to build the phone line used it for free.

Doctors from town sometimes made house calls. They treated the ailments that couldn't be cured by folk remedies. For the most part, Miss Rhody delivered the babies. She was not prideful and would not hesitate to call one of the doctors, if needed.

All able bodied young men were drafted into the service. Those not able bodied or over the maximum accepted age limit did their part at home. Everyone did what they could to help each other.

Many were born and lived through the time of the Southern Reconstruction and were intimately associated with poverty. Immaturity and foolishness had no place in their childhood. They were taught to pay attention and work hard for the survival of their whole family. This mindset was ingrained in them. It was the most valuable thing they owned; and it was inadvertently bequeathed to their offspring.

Chapter 4

Lizzie sat on the back porch peeling potatoes for supper when she saw Charlie walking across the hay meadow towards their neighbor, Mr. Hoots. Charlie had never met him, but that would not deter Charlie because he never met a stranger!

Lizzie wasn't sure if she wanted Charlie associating with Mr. Hoots. He drank sometimes and his reputation preceded him. He was a rowdy, cowboy type, who never saw the necessity to grow up. With Albert gone, Charlie needed male influence. She just wasn't sure if Mr. Hoots would be the best kind of influence. Being in his late sixties had mellowed Mr. Hoots down a great deal, but he still drank and told a few course jokes.

Using a pitchfork, Mr. Hoots unloaded a wagon full of hay around a standing pole. The object was to walk around the pole, packing it tight, and adding hay until it became a tall hay stack for winter feed. The outer layer of hay served as a barrier that shed rain and preserved the inside of the stack. Once the livestock had eaten all the way around the pole, it resembled a giant mushroom which was supported by the center pole.

Charlie watched with childlike curiosity as the stranger worked, but had no idea what he was trying to accomplish. From Charlie's perspective, the man unloaded the hay from the wagon and threw it against the tall pole with hardly any results. With every fork full of hay, he stomped it flat, until he had piled the whole wagon load around the base of the pole.

Charlie yelled to the stranger, "Hey mister, it would be easier to bury that pole if you laid it down!"

The stranger looked up to see a little, dark haired, boy standing there shirtless and barefooted, with a summer tan, and his hands deep down in the pockets of his denim overalls; his shoulders and head were slightly cocked back with his eyebrows raised, as if he was waiting for a response from the old man!

Mr. Hoots chuckled at the little boy: "You must be Albert's boy?! How old are you son?"

"I'm six and a half. Do you know my daddy?" responded Charlie.

"Sure I do. We've been neighbors longer than you've been alive." Mr. Hoots held out his hand for Charlie to shake. Charlie shook his hand and looked him straight in the eye just like he had seen the men do at Miss Rhody's church. He noticed that there was something special, even honorable, in a proper handshake. It had to be done just right or you wouldn't be accepted by the recipient.

Mr. Hoots said, "My name is Roy Hoots." Charlie reciprocated with, "I'm Charlie Pickle."

Mr. Hoots was a prankster, but Charlie hadn't learned that yet. Everyone in the community always said, "That Roy is a hoot!" Some said, "That Roy Hoots don't give a hoot if the sun don't shine!" And some had a few other choice things to say about him as well.

However, the two formed a bond that day and Charlie addressed him as "Mr. Roy." Lizzie expected her children to address adults in a respectful manner. They were always expected to say, "Ma'am" or "Sir" when spoken to by an adult. This show of respect was not so much for the adults benefit, but it was to teach the children how to be humble and respectful. Those were two traits her father had passed down in his family.

Time passed so slowly. Albert was originally drafted to serve a year and a half. Then, President Roosevelt increased service requirements to two and a half years. Later, he signed a decree that increased service requirements again.

This time, it was for the duration of the war, plus six months. Lizzie and Albert were both terribly disappointed.

The children were growing up without Albert. Enna was almost three and Charlie was about to turn seven. They both had grown so much! Charlie was able to help with some of the chores around the house. He kept firewood on the porch in the winter and stove wood for daily cooking stacked in the breezeway near the kitchen.

Because of Albert's absence and Stanley Fletcher's death, Uncle Thomas cut and hauled wood for Lizzie and for Miss Rhody. Uncle Thomas also saw a need for Charlie to have male influence, so he asked Lizzie for permission to teach the boy about cutting and hauling wood. Charlie was taught how to load firewood onto a slide, which is the same thing as a sled, except a slide is used on dirt where a sled is used on snow. There was no need to own a sled in Mississippi. There was no snow, only mud; and a slide worked perfectly in the mud.

Uncle Thomas also taught Charlie mule language. When he yelled, "Gee," the mule turned right. When he yelled, "Haw," the mule turned left. When he yelled, "Whoa," the mule stopped. When he made a clucking sound, the mule went forward. Charlie was amazed! He told Uncle Thomas, "I didn't even know a mule could talk!"

It wasn't long before Lizzie looked up from her work to see Charlie sliding up to the wood pile sitting on top of a stack of wood and yell, "Whoa Nelly!" She thought, "Very impressive skill for a grown man, much less a seven year old child!"

In all the ways that mattered, Charlie was still just a little boy. But Uncle Thomas was stretching his perspective by emphasizing the importance of striving for maturity. He told him, "If you focus on being a child all your life, then that is what you will be in the end. But, if you begin to focus on being a man, you will grow into one!"

Chapter 5

Lizzie sat in the breezeway shelling peas, as a cool zephyr wafted over her, providing a little relief from the heat. She could hear Charlie and Enna talking under the porch where they crawled to play in the cool dirt.

Enna asked Charlie in her, not yet relinquished, baby language, "Where babies come from?" Being the big man that he was, Charlie gave his best, matter of fact, analysis on the subject: "I'm pretty sure they come from under rocks, sorta like them salamanders at the creek. Momma crawled under a rock to hide from a tornado and that's when she found you!"

Enna yelled from under the porch, "Momma, you find me under a rock?" Lizzie answered, "I sure did honey." Enna was quiet for a moment and then asked another question, "Where you find Charlie?" Lizzie contemplated briefly and then said, "Oh, I saw a toad lay an egg beside the back steps and I put it under a setting hen at the barn. Three weeks later, after it hatched, here came Charlie wondering up to the house wanting something to eat. He was so adorable, I decided to keep him!" Charlie quipped back,

"Awe, momma, everybody knows a baby can't walk right after he's hatched!"

Charlie spent a lot of time visiting his new friend, Mr. Roy. He kept him spellbound talking about his old cowboy days.

As a young man, he worked on a very large ranch. He told Charlie about riding broncs and roping calves for branding. He told him how he and a bunch of cowboys moved a giant herd all the way across Texas! Charlie was mesmerized by the stories. He dreamed of being a cowboy like Mr. Roy!

Charlie and Mr. Roy sat under the big oak tree in Mr. Roy's front yard. The straight back chairs creaked as the two leaned back and forth while talking. The heat caused sweat to bead up on their foreheads and also to roll down the crease of their backs.

Mr. Roy licking his lips said, "Boy, my mouth is dry! You want a beer son?" Roy was proba- bly about Charlie's age when his daddy gave him his first beer. Charlie responded, "No Sir! My momma don't allow me to drink beer!" Mr. Roy shrugged and said, "Too bad!— Well, how about a glass of iced tea then?" Charlie indicat- ed by nodding, "Yes Sir! I could drink a whole pitcher by myself!" Roy went into the house and returned with a cold beer and a cold glass of tea for his new little buddy.

Charlie noticed that Mr. Roy's thumb was missing from his right hand, and asked, "Mr. Roy? I've been meaning to ask. What happened to your thumb?" Even though Charlie wanted to be a cowboy, there was a lot that he still didn't know or understand about the actual job. While lassoing stock, many cowboys lose their thumbs and fingers, if they are not careful. They must dally their ropes around the horn of the saddle very quickly and sometimes their entangled digits get snipped off. It is a very fast and painful amputation and that is what happened to Roy's thumb. However, Roy mischievously began to weave a tall tale for his gullible young friend.

"You see Charlie, me and the boys were on a long cattle drive across the desert. We had no water. Everybody was dying of thirst. The cows were thirsty and the horses were thirsty. Suddenly, we looked on the horizon and could see a patch of trees. Well, we knew if there was trees, there would be water. So, we turned the herd toward the trees. After a long hot day, we finally got there and sure enough, in the middle of those trees was the prettiest pool of water you ever saw! It was cold and blue like the ocean!—

Well! Everybody fell on their faces slurping up that water. Man it was good!— About that time a giant alligator jumped up out of the water and ate the fellow next to me!— Before we could back up from the watering hole, more alligators ate all the rest of the boys!— I fell back quick enough and hid behind a tree. But when I looked down, my thumb was missing. One of them alligators had snapped it off before I knew it! — Well, I ran and got on my horse and drove them cattle back away from the pool and out of the trees. I guess those alligators lived off of poor unsuspecting victims who come to get water. Since I was the only one left, I drove that herd of cows all the way to Texas by myself!"

Charlie was on the edge of his seat as he sipped the cold tea and watched Mr. Roy spin his story. His eyes were big as saucers and the more he leaned forward listening, the more animated Mr. Roy became.

That night Charlie dreamed that his momma sent him to the spring to get a bucket of water. When he dipped the bucket into the spring, a giant alligator jumped out of the water and swallowed his bucket! Charlie struggled to run through The Hardwoods trying to escape the giant alligator. But his legs were so heavy, as if they didn't want to work! His heart pounded with fear!

Suddenly, he felt pressure in his bladder. He urgently needed to go. Charlie watched intently for the giant alligator as he stepped behind a large tree and went.

That's when Charlie awoke from his dream. His bed clothes and everything else in the bed were ringing wet. Charlie had wet the bed.

He climbed out of bed. His heart was still pounding, but he was relieved to learn that his legs were working. Charlie was also relieved to discover that it was only a dream.

Removing the wet pajamas, he pulled dry clothes out of the chest of drawer and put them on. Then, he grabbed the extra blanket that was neatly folded on the end of his bed and curled up on the floor.

His momma was surprised the next morning to find Charlie sleeping on the floor and his bed wet.

"He was too old to be wetting the bed," she mumbled to herself. She gently shook Charlie awake and said, "You had a little accident last night, didn't you buddy?" Charlie's deep slumber was replaced by conscious confusion, "Huh?" Then Charlie remembered the dream. He was too embarrassed to tell his momma what really happened. He just said, "I drank too much tea at Mr. Roy's yesterday."

Chapter 6

The greyhound bus pulled to the side of the highway and stopped. The passenger doors swung open and off stepped a soldier with his duffel bag hanging from his shoulder. He marched down the hill towards the crossroads.

It was a beautiful spring day so Lizzie and the children had gone to the crossroads to look for fossils in the gravel. The long silver bus sitting still on the highway caught Lizzie's attention. She saw a tall slender man with broad shoulders marching towards them, with a long green bag suspended from his square shoulder.

The children were oblivious of the approaching soldier as they continued to look through the gravel for fossils, but Lizzie's heart pounded with anticipation as she contemplated the possibility that this tall figure marching towards them could be her husband! If this was him, he was much thinner than she remembered, but those broad shoulders looked like his. As he approached, Lizzie recognized Albert's dark complexion, blue eyes, and dark hair. His gait seemed different, almost mechanical. The corners of her mouth began to turn upwards to match his as she screamed, "Albert!" The startled children looked up from their search to see their mother run into the open arms of a stranger standing in the road. With apprehension, the two children approached the couple, now shamelessly kissing for everybody to see!

After what seemed like a lifetime, the two lovebirds unlocked and Lizzie brought Albert's attention to the two children awkwardly standing a few paces away. "Buddy, come over here and greet your daddy." Charlie was just over three years old when Albert left. He barely remembered him in person, but he knew him by the letters that his momma read to him and Enna.

Charlie extended his right hand and said, "Hello sir." Albert reached for his hand and swooped him up all in one motion. "How ya been Buddy?! You've doubled in size, since I saw you last!"

Enna slowly crept to her mother's hind side where she hugged her momma's leg like a tree and shyly peeked around her skirt at the stranger. Albert spied her and said, "Where is my Enna Marie?! I have been dying to meet my beautiful little girl!" Lizzie stepped aside while detaching Enna from her leg. "Come around baby and meet your daddy!"

Albert swept her up into his unoccupied strong arm and kissed her on the cheek. She blushed and turned her head away. "She is teased!" Said Albert. Then, he carefully lowered them both to the ground as he excitedly announced, "Hey! I've got something for both of you!" The two children looked on with anticipation as their father unfolded the top of his duffle bag. In it, was a stack of neatly folded clothes, topped off by four carefully placed wooden animals. He reached in and picked up two cows, complete with horns, and handed them to Charlie, saying, "Here Buddy, your momma told me that you like horses and cows. I hope you like these. I carved them from a piece of driftwood that I found on the beach." Charlie beamed with pride as his father handed him the toys. The realization that his daddy was thinking about him in that far away place made him feel warm inside.

Albert knelt on one knee in the gravel. The expression on his son's face made him smile. Charlie gazed and marveled at the two cows, then hugged his daddy in appreciation and deep love.

Albert's attention then turned to Enna. She stood beside him stretching to see the interaction between him and Charlie.

The sun shimmered from her black hair. The olive complexion of her skin was accented by the early spring tan that she and Charlie both had acquired from the exposure to outdoor life. Her beautiful blue eyes stared in wonderment at Charlie's cows as she speculated on the treasure that could be hers. Then, she shrieked with joy as Albert presented her with two wooden figurines from his bag. "What are they?" She asked. Albert said, "They are lambs; sweet and innocent just like you!"

Enna held the little lambs very delicately as if they would break. "I love lambs! I am naming them Clara and Max!" When she fell into her daddy's open arms, she said: "And I love you too daddy!"

The remainder of that day was spent on the porch. Albert and Lizzie sat side by side in the swing like two newfound young lovers as Charlie and Enna hovered about them, playing with their new toys and asking their father questions about where he had been and what he had seen.

Albert told them about the places he had been and the people he had met, but he never talked about the war, not that day or any day thereafter. Although the graphic memories were permanently imprinted in his mind and haunted him, he left them there.

"Enough questions you two! It's two hours past your bedtime. You have a whole lifetime to talk to your father!" Lizzie declared. Their father kissed them goodnight and they scampered off to bed.

The early spring evening was cool, too cool for porch sitting, but that didn't stop the two lovebirds from making up for lost time.

After seeing the kids to bed, Lizzie showed up on the porch with two hot cups of coffee: "Thought you might want something to warm your insides." She handed Albert his cup and reached through the open window for her momma's quilt that she stored in a chair just inside.

Over the past four years, she spent many lonely nights sitting out in the swing, wrapped up in her momma's quilt, wondering about her husband. How he was doing? When would he be home? If he would be home?

She set her coffee down on the table in front of the swing. She wrapped one end of the quilt around Albert's shoulder. Then, while reaching for her coffee, before nestling close beside him, she pulled the other end of the quilt around her own shoulders.

The night air cloaked with perfume brought memories to mind of their wedding night. Lizzie's fully developed beauty transcended the mere attractiveness of the young girl he left behind four years before. Moonlight shone across her face, accentuating her soft olive complexion, contrasted by perfectly shaped, red painted lips and dove like eyes framed by thick dark lashes.

Albert held her delicate hand. She laid her head on his strong shoulder; her back rested against his powerful, brawny torso making her feel warm and safe. Her soft closeness made him feel happy and blessed.

The swing swayed gently, carrying them together, back and forth; their hearts intertwined into one heart, one soul, one dream. Both of them desiring to always be passionately in love and to never forget this moment.

The next day Lizzie opened all the windows, changed all the beds, and scrubbed the floors. Springtime brought spring fever. She loved to let the fresh air flow through the house. It made everything smell fresh and clean.

Albert made a list of all the things that needed to be done. The first thing on his list was to get the old truck running. Since Lizzie didn't drive, the truck had been sitting idle in the barn over the last four years.

Stanley Fletcher made a gift of the truck to Albert and Lizzie for their first wedding anniversary. It held sentimental value, and he needed a new truck for his business.

Albert opened the gas cap, bent over and sniffed the tank. The gas was definitely old. He would have to drain the tank. Next, he raised the hood. Dirt daubers and wasp nests coated the underside of it. Due to a cool spring season, the nests were unoccupied. So, he pulled them loose and threw them on the ground. Mud daubers were under the breather cap also. The spark plug wires were brittle and cracked. "Probably needed plugs too!" Albert thought. "I might as well change the oil and filter while I'm at it."

Albert walked the three miles into town to get parts. Three miles was nothing after marching across Europe. Besides, it gave him time to organize his thoughts and plan the work that needed to be done.

After Lizzie shared with him the circumstances of Enna's birth, he didn't want his family going to the spring much longer to get water. He planned to dig a well. But first he had to buy a mule for spring planting. And before he could do that, he had to repair the fence that was destroyed by the tornado four years prior. By late that evening, he had repaired the truck.

"One thing off the list!" He told Lizzie as he grabbed a bar of soap and a towel. "I'm headed to the spring to take a bath."

The next day was sale day at the stockyard and Albert needed livestock for the farm. Charlie stayed home from school so he could go to the sale with his family. He had never been to one before and was excited.

They sat together in the bleachers listening to the gibberish coming from the auctioneer. "Do I hear ten dollars? Bibita bibita bibita Hup! ten dollars. Now do I hear ten-fifty? Ten-fifty? Ten fifty? biibitibibiti bibiti...ten twenty-five? Can I get ten-twenty five? Bibiti bibiti bibiti sold! Ten dollars to number sixteen." Charlie naively looked at his father and said, "Gosh! Enna could talk better than that when she was two!"

It happened to be one of those strange moments when the room was perfectly quiet and a loud cackle echoed throughout the building at Charlie's innocent observation. However, Charlie was unaware that the laughter in the building was due to his comment and continued his discourse, "Daddy, why does the man talk like that?" Albert smiled at his son's innocence and said, "He does that to build excitement in the crowd so they will bid higher."

In the middle of Albert's explanation, a gentle but stocky mule plodded into the ring along with a female donkey and her colt. He had already inspected the mule before the sale and knew she would go for a premium because she was young and well bred. He had no use for the donkey, colt pair and he was certain nobody else did either. They had no real value and he was certain she and her colt were only thrown in with the high quality mule to get rid of her.

The auctioneer began the bidding at fifty dollars. Albert flashed his card and the auctioneer pointed at him while looking intently across the room.

"I got fifty dollars, bibiti bibiti bibiti do I hear sixty? bibiti bibiti bibiti...

In the back row, a Jewish man wearing a kippah, flashed his card after his wife nudged him and pointed at the auctioneer.

Albert recognized the man and his wife as Phineas and Penelope Bartholomew, who owned the drug store in town. Earlier when Albert walked to the back pens to inspect the mule, they were already there looking through the fence at the animals while having a serious, but urgent conversation. Their suspicious dis-

cussion ended quickly and they walked away after seeing Albert approaching the pen.

Penelope was not Jewish by heritage. In
fact, she came from English stock and was a
native of Misty Hollow. She was a beautiful, but
frail looking woman who held a fretting baby up
to her shoulder lightly patting its back in an attempt to calm its agitation. She seemed bossy
and kept an anxious expression on her face at all
times. Phineas, on the other hand, was a small
statured man with an ambivalent personality.

"Hup! I got sixty! sixty dollars, sixty dollars,
sixty dollars. Do I hear seventy? bibiti bibiti
bibiti...

Albert sat up straighter in his seat and
cocked his head vertically one quick jerk, signal-
ing the auctioneer to raise the bid. He complied
and then yelled in excitement to the man on the
back row, "Alright friend! I got a bid of seventy
dollars! Can I get eighty? bibiti bibiti bibiti..."

The man looked at the woman, who sternly
looked back at him inducing him to nervously
flash his card.

"Hup!"
The auctioneer looked again at Albert after
scanning the crowd in search of any new bid-
ders.

"We've got eighty! Do I hear ninety? bibiti
bibiti bibiti...
Albert lifted his eyebrows causing the auctioneer
to take notice and eagerly yell to the crowed,
"Ninty dollars!"
The going price for a mule was about $80 so the
new higher bid motivated the auctioneer to carefully gather bids almost like he was the judge at
a marshmallow stacking contest! He again
looked at the guy on the back row,
    "Friend I've got Ninty! Do I hear a hundred?
Can you go a hundred? bibiti bibiti bibiti bibiti
bibiti bibiti... Come on friend, it's just money!
bibiti bibiti bibiti... Ninty going once...!"
The nervous man looked kind of sick, but after
his stern faced wife glared at him, he flashed the
card again anyway.
Albert stared at Phineas in disbelief and thought,
"Why would anybody in his right mind bid a
hundred dollars on a mule when he could buy
one any day of the week for eighty dollars?"
    The auctioneer stood up and took his micro-
phone in hand as he loosened his western style
bow tie enough to allow blood circulation
through his over expanded jugular veins.
    "I've got a hundred! Let me hear one ten!
bibiti bibiti bibiti bibiti..."
Lizzie grabbed Albert's arm and pleaded,

"Albert, please, no!"
Albert whispered to Lizzie,
   "This is the only mule at the sale and I'm not going home without her!"
The now animated auctioneer stood on his tip-toes pointing hard at Albert.
   "Mister, I've got a hundred, can you give one hundred and ten dollars?"
Albert defiantly glared at Phineas on the back row and yelled,
   "One Ten!"
The crowd shrieked in astonishment, and the auctioneer removed his cowboy hat to wipe dripping sweat from his forehead. The blood veins
bulged in his temples causing his whole face to turn red while continuing the bid.
   "I've got one hundred and ten dollars. Do I hear one twenty?
The little man sorrowfully looked back at Albert and raised his card. Penelope removed her attention from her husband and stared Albert down, until he could do nothing, but shamefully look at the floor.
   The auctioneer was spastic as he bellowed over the loud chatter erupting throughout the large arena:

"I got one hundred and twenty dollars! A donkey family and a mule, all for the same money! Can I get one thirty? Bid on the whole set for one thirty! bibiti bibiti bibiti...

Albert never looked up and yelled,

"One thirty!"

Before the the auctioneer could offer the next bid, the agitated woman stood up with her baby and yelled,

"Two hundred and fifty Dollars!"

The auctioneer stripped his tie from his neck and threw his hat up into the air in disbelief at the obviously eccentric couple and their puny baby on the back row! Nobody anywhere in the world would pay that kind of money for these animals unless they were absent of their faculties. After collecting himself, the auctioneer continued the bid.

"Okay folks, we have a bid of two hundred and fifty dollars on the whole set. Is there anyone out there who can bid two sixty? bibiti bibiti bibiti...Two sixty bibiti bibiti bibiti..."

Albert was careful to control his eyebrows and everyone else remained perfectly still. None of them wanted the auctioneer to mistake any of their movements for a bid because that kind of money was way out of all their budgets.

"Two fifty going once, going twice. Sold to the nice lady in the back row!"

Everyone in the arena were astonished by the strange behavior of the city folks who bought the mules, but none were as dumbfounded as Albert. He really needed the young mule to work his fields, but he wasn't going home empty handed. By the end of the sale, he had managed to by three jersey milk cows along with three sows and a boar hog. He would just have to find a mule some place else.

The last animal to come through the sale was a scrawny old horse with tall withers and a long head. By then, the auctioneer had re-adorned his hat and tie. His constricted blood vessels had returned to their natural size and he spoke plain English describing the rough looking snag standing in the middle of the ring.

"Now folks, this horse ain't no bad horse! He just needs some groceries! Here's a good opportunity to get a fine horse at a cheap price! I'm gonna start the bidding at five dollars!"

Albert got up to leave, but Charlie grabbed his hand with both of his while jumping up and down. He looked at his daddy with pleading eyes begging quickly,

"Please! Please! Please!"

Now Albert wasn't no dummy! He knew that this was the universal language for little boys that meant, "I want this horse!"

The gibberish had started, but not the bids. Albert yelled to the auctioneer,

"How old is that horse?"
The auctioneer stopped his gibberish and asked a man in the ring,

"Sam, look in that horse's mouth and see how old he is?" Sam looked and and replied, "Looks to be twelve." The auctioneer repeated and said,

"The horse is twelve years old. Who'll give five dollars? Bibiti bibiti bibiti... How about four dollars? Who'll give me four dollars? Bibiti bibiti bibiti..." Charlie squeezed his father's hand really tight and it seemed to caused his other hand to go up in the air. The auctioneer acknowledged Albert's bid and then bellowed,

"Alright, we got four dollars. Can we get four and a quarter? Four and a quarter? Bibiti bibiti bibiti...going once, going twice, sold! To number twenty-two! For four dollars!"

Charlie was the proudest and most excited person at the sale. He told his momma, "Mr Roy ain't going to believe it when I come riding up on my new horse! I'm gonna name him Buck!"

When Albert went to the cashier to pay for his livestock, he saw Phineas with Penelope holding her sickly baby and waiting near the counter. They no longer seemed competitive or anxious, but they did act like they were waiting for Albert.

Phineas held out his hand in a friendly gesture and said, "Albert, I'm sorry for all the ruckus in there, but now I can explain what was going on. Do you have a minute?" Albert was intrigued by the offer of Phineas to explain the mysterious interaction. So, he listened intently. "You probably noticed that we are out of our element at a livestock sale." Albert nodded in agreement. Then, Phineas continued, "Well, let me start at the beginning. Our little Arabella..." he said while pointing at the baby in Penelope's arms, "...is allergic to milk. That includes her mother's milk. She can hardly keep any of it on her stomach. The doctors have done everything they can to help and offer no solution to the problem. As you can see, she is very thin and getting thinner every day. Anyway, one morning, I mentioned our problem to one of our customers, Miss Butterfield Morgan, who has helped birth most of the black babies in three counties. She came from a long line of African doulas and midwives dating back to the seventeen hundreds and before. They have used unconventional techniques for centuries with extraordinary success. Well, without even a stutter she said, "Donkey's milk; all you need is donkey's milk!"

Well Albert, do you know how hard it is to find a lactating donkey in Mississippi? We have put up fliers all over town and been to every livestock sale within a hundred miles. When we finally saw there was a donkey at this sale today we were so relieve, but we were also afraid that someone else would buy the donkey out from under us.

Albert, as you can see, we don't need the grown mule and if you will take the mule, half of my problem will be solved." Albert responded, "I would definitely be glad to take the mule off of your hands, but what is the other half of your problem?" Phineas perplexing threw his arms in the air and exclaimed, "I've got to figure out how to milk a donkey!"

Since the tornado destroyed the fence, it was Charlie's job to tether the animals out to graze each day. Every morning, he tethered the horse and mule out first and when Albert finished milking, Charlie tethered them out also. The hogs were kept in a stall temporarily, until a pen could be built. The fence was broken down in several places, but Albert had it repaired in a few days. The Black Locust posts were cut by his grandfather and were still solid as a rock and also as hard as a rock!

The cows, the horse, and the mule were then turned together into the pasture. They bucked and kicked in celebration before burying their muzzles in the tender green grass.

Albert drove to the sawmill and picked up a load of free slabs for a pigpen. Slabs are the edgings cut from the log and the sawer was always glad to see someone come along and get them out if his way.

The hogs were happy to be released from the dusty stall of the barn also. They immediately began rooting in the dirt and eating grass. It wouldn't be long before the sows would have pigs, producing meat and income.

The milk truck stopped each morning to pick up the single can of milk that Albert left at the road. His three cows produced enough milk for their household with plenty to sell. Lizzie made butter and buttermilk from any that started to go bad at home.

The chickens had been free ranging and multiplying since Albert left for the service. There was never a shortage of fried chicken on Lizzie's table.

In fact, Enna had developed a keen taste for chicken legs. Some people called them drum-sticks, but Enna just called them legs. It was nothing for Lizzie to grab a chicken and ring it's neck while going to or from the clothesline. Charlie and Enna saw it all the time. It was as natural as going to the cub-bard for a can of beans.

Finally, it was time for Charlie to learn the ways of chicken killing and plucking. Lizzie sent the children out to find a fat, juicy chicken for supper. Charlie had a difficult time picking out the fattest and juiciest chicken on the yard, but Enna was growing weary of the search. Then Charlie said, "What about that one Enna? Does it look fat and juicy?" Fully exasperated, Enna replied, "I don't know which one to get! Just get the one with the most legs!"

According to the Almanac, the Spring Equinox was past and it was time to plant the garden. After Albert finished planting the corn, Lizzie told him about how uncle Thomas had taught Charlie to handle a mule and slide. That's when Albert decided it was a good time to make him familiar with plowing too.

Charlie picked it up easily. He had a way with the mule, who was named in honor of Penelope Bartholomew, since she left a lasting impression on all of them. Albert stood on one knee at the end of every row for a guide to help Charlie keep the rows straight.

Charlie spoke mule language to Penelope, using his deep and authoritative voice. "Whoa Penelope!" The mule stopped at the end of the row as Charlie leaned the plow over to extract it from the earth. "Haw! — Haw!" Penelope then turned right to start another row.

Albert was proud of his son. At four and a half feet tall, weighing sixty pounds, Charlie would obviously one day be a big man. He was stocky like his father and wasn't afraid of work. Uncle Thomas had taught him well

Chapter 7

Albert pitched another spade of dirt into the homemade wheelbarrow. His head was all that Lizzie could see poking out of a hole that he created in the middle of the breezeway floor.

"You got that well dug yet?" Said Lizzie facetiously. He retorted,

"Naw, I've dug down six inches and still ain't hit water!"

Uncle Thomas' laugh drifted from under the house as he acknowledged both of them with a remark of his own,

"I came up here to work, but it looks like I got a front row seat to a comedy show instead!" Albert retorted,

"I bet neither of us will be laughing by the time this job is finished!"

The very old log house, complete with dog trot, was left to Albert when his parents died. The house was constructed from virgin pine logs harvested along the ridge above Misty Hollow. His ancestors hewed the logs by hand shortly after venturing into North Central Mississippi. The pioneer home consisted of two bedrooms on one side of the breezeway and a bedroom and parlor on the other side. A kitchen built off the rear of the left side created a second breezeway and prevented summer cooking from heating the remainder of the house.

Each generation living in the house had become so accustomed to carrying water up the hill from the spring that they probably did not realize the inconvenience; or maybe well construction was so much different in times past that it was more inconvenient to build one. There were no concrete curbings in those days so the sides would have been dug square and framed with lumber which eventually would rot away allowing collapse and re-construction.

Albert planned for the new well to be accessible in the center of the back porch in line with the main breezeway. He removed the root cellar door, making it possible to roll the wheelbarrow right up to the place where the well was to be dug.

A load of concrete well tiles were delivered and rolled into position. A well tile is a short section of concrete pipe designed to stack and interlock together. Uncle Thomas inserted them into the well. The stack descended into the hole as Albert dug beneath the bottom tile. This process continued until they hit water.

Uncle Thomas extracted the dirt as Albert delivered it to the top of the well using a bucket attached to a block and tackle. Thirty tiles and three weeks later, Albert let out a muffled squeal from the sixty foot hole in the ground. Uncle Thomas cupped his hand to his ear and yelled into the dark hole, "You hit China yet?" Albert yelled upward, "I missed the mainland, but I knocked a hole in the bottom of the ocean, cause it's flooding in!"

He hitched his harness and pulled himself out of the well. The dim light in the breezeway was enough to make him squint his eyes, but the warm air felt good to his bones. He had been in the ground so long, he felt like a prairie dog!

After another day of work, the carpentry of the frame and wench supports were completed around the mouth of the well and extended upward through the breezeway floor to the level of waist high. Then Albert asked, "What do I owe you Uncle Thomas?" Uncle Thomas replied, "You don't owe me anything now, but you can help me make molasses when my cane is ready." Albert gladly responded, "That sounds like a good trade. Just holler at me when you are ready." Then he jokingly added, "I'll trade you a bucket of well water for a bucket of molasses!"

Chapter 8

Every species of animal on the farm was given a name except the chickens and the hogs. Lizzie's rule was, "You just don't name something that you're going to eat!"

The milk cows, Betsy, Sally and Belle, may or may not have recognized their names; but for certain, they associated sounds with feed and they always came to the barn when Lizzie or Albert called.

Enna possessed a natural female need to talk. Oftentimes, she searched for someone onto which she might unload her plethora of accumulated words. It did not matter whether it was someone or something. Neither did it matter if the object listened. As long as she was able to mindlessly rattle, she was satisfied.

Her favorite place to search for an audience was at the barn where she was able to entice a willing subject with a little corn.

She climbed the first three rungs of the ladder which led to the loft and reached across to unlatch the crib door. While standing inside the open doorway, she pushed the crib door back slowly until it bumped the wall.

The sound of cow bells was heard as the three milk cows raised their heads from grazing in acknowledgment of the door bump. Enna called the cows with her deepest voice, "Sulk, sulk, sulk, come Betsy, come Sally, come Belle."

The cows certainly had no regard for Enna's commands like they did when her momma called them. However, they were very familiar with the sound of the rusty hinges of the crib door, squeaking and popping, as it swung and slammed against the wall. The cows ran from the pasture with their udders swinging back and forth underneath them like a trio of church bells.

They approached the barn, shoulder to shoulder, at a dead run! All three heads thrust into the open crib door in competition as their chests slammed against the bottom of the doorway, causing them to stop abruptly while silencing the clanging bells draped around their necks.

The sudden forceful action caught Enna off guard, throwing her backwards into the pile of corn. She rolled over onto to her knees and stood up glaring at the unruly milk cows. Both clinched fists held an ear of corn and rested on her tiny hips. She shook an ear of corn at the cows and sternly informed them, "Now, if you girls are going to act like hogs, then we're going to un-name you and put you in the hog pen for fattening!"

Chapter 9

Buck was beginning to look more like a race horse and less like the old plug that Albert bought at the stock sale. A few ears of corn every day along with good grass and spring water was all the groceries he needed. Plus, a plug of chewing tobacco for gut worms made him look as healthy as ever.

Charlie sat bareback on the powerful horse as he cantered down the dirt road which led to the old Stennis place. He brought leftover bacon wrapped in a handkerchief for a snack. He thought, "Cowboys always had some jerky when they were on the trail." Continuing with his cowboy fantasy, he told Buck, "We'll camp at the old shack up ahead." There were two pear trees in the front yard and he wanted to give Buck a pear for his sweet tooth.

From a distance, Charlie saw a scrawny dog lying under the tree gnawing on a pear. He wondered whose dog this could be. The house was not on a main road and there was no one living nearby. As Charlie and Buck approached, the dog slinked away and hid under the house. Charlie slid down from the horse's back and slowly slithered under the edge of the porch.

"Come here boy," Charlie said while making a kissing sound with his puckered lips.

The dog remained in the darkness beyond sight. Charlie remembered the bacon in his pocket; as he opened it, the smell of smoked bacon wafted into his nostrils, making him hungry. He spoke into the darkness, "That sure does smell good! You better come and get some or I'm going to eat it by myself!" The aroma of the bacon reached the dogs keen sense of smell and it slowly crawled towards him. The dog's interest in the offering perked Charlie's enthusiasm, prompting him to eagerly creep towards the dog, which caused the dog to retreat back into the darkness. Disappointed, Charlie withdrew from under the house and sat with his back to the dog. He held a piece of bacon behind himself and called again very softly. After a bit, a gentle muzzle removed the bacon from his hand.

Charlie presented another small piece of bacon in the same manner and it was also gently removed from his hand again. Very slowly, he turned to face the dog without looking directly into his eyes. While speaking softly, Charlie offered another bribe. His gentle voice and non-threatening nature was soothing to the frightened dog who began to relax and warm up to Charlie. The stray came close enough for Charlie to touch and softly pet. It wasn't long before the dog realized that Charlie was a friend. And also, it wasn't long before Charlie realized that "he" was a "she".

The dog's skeleton supported her white and black speckled hide like a collapsing circus tent. She had a bird dog look about her and was covered with ticks and fleas.

Apparently, her survival depended on the ripe pears falling from the loaded tree. He offered her the remaining bacon and she swallowed it whole. "Gosh! You didn't even take time to taste it!" Charlie exclaimed.

Charlie mounted the horse by clenching it's mane in both hands. Then with the help of his split toes gripping the tendon above the fetlock, he pulled himself up onto his back. The mutt fell in behind the horse like she belonged. Charlie was glad to see her tagging along and hoped she would be well received at home. By the time they got there, the dog was named after his favorite teacher, Miss Elly Mae Nithercott, who was pretty and always nice.

Lizzie saw Charlie coming out of *The Hardwoods* riding Buck and talking to a scrawny speckled hound that followed close behind. From the fence she yelled, "What is that following you Buddy?" As Charlie approached the fence he said, "This is Elly Mae. I found her at the old Stennis place. She ain't had nothing to eat but pears!"

Lizzie felt pity for the dog. She could see that the worms, fleas, and ticks had just about sucked all the blood out of her. "Buddy, it will be a miracle if this dog lives. The parasites are about to take her!" Charlie was frantic, "Can you help her momma?" Lizzie calmingly said, "First, let's get some food into her. I'll cook a pone of cornbread. Run down to the spring and get a jug of milk. And while your down there pick up some walnut hulls to make a dewormer."

Elly Mae devoured the milk and cornbread which swelled her potbelly out of proportion and caused her bony tail to wag uncontrollably.

Charlie drew two pails of water from the well and poured them into the wash tub. The contented but oblivious dog lay in the grass licking her foot, when Charlie picked her up by the chest and carefully placed her in the the cold bath water. Afterwards, she ran into hiding under the house, leaving the tub filled with dead fleas and ticks.

Lizzie sent Buddy to the root cellar for a few cloves of garlic to be used in the homemade dog dewormer. By the time he returned, she had grated the walnut hulls into powder. When she added the garlic, Charlie reacted by pinching his nose and exclaiming, "Feww-eee!-That stinks!" Lizzie confirmed it, "Yea! We gotta' get this con-coction into Elly Mae for those worms!"

Once Elly Mae saw Charlie dump the wash-tub and put it away, she felt safe and came out from under the house. Charlie enticed her with a sweet comforting voice and then held her as Lizzie straddled her back. While holding the roof of her mouth, she dipped two fingers into the concoction and pasted it on the back of Elly Mae's tongue. The skinny dog fought furiously to escape as Lizzie clamped and held her mouth shut, until she swallowed the nasty tasting folk medicine. After swallowing, the routine was re-peated two more times for good measure, and then she was released.

Perplexed by what she perceived as rough treatment, Elly Mae once again scrambled under the house where she remained for a while, until she realized that Charlie had gone about his business and was not concerned with her. In a few weeks, she began to bloom. The color came back into her skin and she gained weight. Her beautiful coat glimmered in the sun. She became playful realizing that Charlie had saved her life.

Chapter 10

The cultivator creaked and popped in response to the intense stress placed on it by the powerful mule as she effortlessly pulled the plow down each row. There was a mundane sound of chains rattling and roots tearing under the earth as Albert plodded along behind the plow. Each sweep rolled the soil like waves, dislodging the grass and weeds, creating a soft, damp furrow between the rows. Birds flew from the trees to gather worms and grubs as they were unearthed and exposed to the sunshine. A single pass from one end of the field to the other, being a quarter mile in length, was doubled by the time both sides of the row were plowed.

The tedious, but mesmerizing work caused Albert's thoughts to wander back in time to old memories of the once special people in his life. His father-in-law, Rosemond Stuckey, was one of those people. Albert held him in the highest regard because he was a man of integrity and honor, who was a good father to Lizzie and her brothers.

Mrs. Stuckey died when the children were very young; he raised them in a godly home, do-ing the very best that he could.

Albert was entertained by his wandering thoughts. He remembered the day Mr. Stuckey drove the wagon for him, while he pulled corn. The field was new ground, which had previously been pasture, dotted about with a tree here and there. The trees were removed, leaving the stumps tall enough so that they were visible and could be avoided when plowing and planting; but, they were short enough to miss the wagon's axle. However, when the corn grew tall and thick, the stumps were hidden from view.

During the harvest, it was common practice to drive over the dried stalks as the corn was hand pulled and loaded into the wagon. Mr. Stuckey drove the wagon responding to Albert's instructions to pull forward, as needed. As He clucked and snapped the reigns, the mule pulled forward and tripped over a hidden stump. The surprise of stumbling blindly over the immovable object, startled the mule. She bolted with the wagon and Mr. Stuckey, who was sitting in a re-laxed position, with his feet propped up against the front of the wagon. His back was bowed, allowing his elbows to rest on his knees, while holding the reigns. Lurching forward, the wagon reached the hidden stump, which had not been cut short enough. It caught the axle, bringing the whole rig to a jolting stop, that is - everything except Mr. Stuckey! He flew in the air past the front of the wagon, end over end, arthritically frozen in a sitting position and landed upright on the mule, as if he had been sitting there all along! The mule wasn't happy about receiving an instant passenger on its back, so she stepped out from under him. Mr. Stuckey hit the ground with a thud and a groan.

Seeing the commotion, but unable to re-spond quickly enough, Albert rushed to rescue him from under the mule, which by now was vio-lently snorting and attempting to yank the wagon over the stump!

After removing Mr. Stuckey from danger, Al-bert settled the mule and untangled the mess made by the hidden stump. Mr. Stuckey pulled himself together and hobbled to the house where he decided that he needed a break from farm work. The next day, he caught the bus to Alabama to visit his little brother. Poor Lizzie never saw him again.

Thinking about Lizzie's parents caused Albert to remember his own: Paul and Julia Pickle. They were wonderful people. His momma was a godly woman who never missed church. His fa-ther was a good man; but, he hated church. He always said, "Everybody down there at that place are just too stuffy!"

Most Sundays you could find him at a lake somewhere fishing. When he wasn't fishing, he was hauling cattle for the local stockyards. Daddy Paul was in demand because he owned his own two ton cattle truck with stake sides. The truck was used to haul every kind of live-stock; but, sometimes it was used for more practical purposes, like weekend fishing trips.

Once Albert was old enough, he was allowed to go with his father and uncles fishing on an oxbow lake near the Mississippi River. They bragged about the catfish being so plentiful, you had to knock them out of the way just so you could get upstream.

Since Albert had never gone fishing with the crew before, he thought that some of the their gear seemed a little strange for a fishing trip. The inventory consisted of: a large homemade chest type cooler made from boards and saw-dust for insulation, a few buckets of trot lines, six fishing poles, a tackle box, a few groceries, cooking supplies, seven blankets, a couple of lanterns, three heavy oak boards the length of the truck-bed, a coffee can full of sixty penny nails, and six sharp axes.

Not everyone could ride in the cab. Rear passengers were determined by age and maturity level. The front seat was reserved for the driver and two older, less adventurous occupants. The two hour ride in the back of the cattle truck would have been long and tiring if not for the entertainment. The heavy springs turned the unloaded truck into a giant catapult for anyone brave enough to walk past the rear axle to the end of the bed. His uncles competed to see who could stand the longest before losing their balance. Anyone who lost their balance, bounced around on the floor uncontrollably, unable to regain any composure. Finally, when they were bored with that competition, they began to see who could get up from the floor the fastest, which wasn't humanly possible unless they bumped into the stake sides and could get a grip on the slats!

Upon arrival, every man picked up an axe and started cutting logs. Using the logs, oak boards, and spikes, they built a raft. Albert was impressed by his uncles as they completed the project in less than an hour.

Daddy Paul sent Albert to scratch for bait, while the grownups built the raft. Along the bank, buried under the wet leaves, was found an abundance of worms the size of small snakes.

Albert cautiously filled a five gallon bucket with worms and moist leaves, making sure that none of the worms had heads or rattles.

By mid morning, everything was loaded onto the homemade raft. They pushed away from the bank using push poles found in a drift. Some of his uncles managed the fishing poles and stringing trot lines, while the others navigated the large bulky craft.

Although lunch time came and went without any fanfare, they all had their fill of hoop cheese and bologna on saltine crackers, washed down with an ice cold soda pop from the homemade wooden cooler. By supper time, they pulled up on a large sandbar and set up camp. The lanterns hung from two forked poles buried upright in the sand on either side of the fire at a far enough distance to cast a dim, soft light. Catfish, hush puppies, and fresh cut French fries were cooked over an open fire. During the evening, hilarious joke telling and exuberant laughter were enjoyed by all.

The trot lines were checked throughout the night while Albert slept peacefully on the soft bed of sand. The next morning, Albert was awakened by the smell of bacon and the noise of gear being loaded onto the raft. After camp was broken up, they slothfully took turns push poling the raft back to the site of the waiting cattle truck, where the gear and supply of catfish were loaded for the return trip home.

Daddy Paul drove in solitude next to the exhausted front passengers, who laid their heads on each other's shoulders and slept all the way home. The rear passengers sat near the cab nodding off, too tired to play games. The homemade raft was abandoned on the shore where perhaps some other fishing party could make use of it until the Mississippi River flooded the lake and washed it into the Gulf of Mexico.

The mule suddenly stopped, interrupting Albert's memories momentarily. A sinkhole the size of a man had formed at the end of the row, near the creek, and the mule stood still, waiting for Albert's direction. After maneuvering the mule around the obstacle and getting her started down the next row, renewed monotony sent his mind back into the past.

The sink hole reminded him of the fox holes that he and cousin Eddy had dug during the war. Once, they dug a two man hole and were trapped there for days by heavy enemy fire. A platoon of enemy tanks rolled through in an attempt to collapse the foxholes and dislodge them from their position.

A tank placed its tracks directly over their foxhole and spun in circles; digging and spreading dirt back into the hole until they were almost buried alive. The whole time this was happening to them, Eddy was praying out loud, "Lord, I don't care about me cause I am yours, but please spare Albert!"

Miraculously, the tank stopped spinning on top of them and moved on to the next foxhole, where the occupants were crushed to death.

During the days before their foxhole collapsed, Eddy told Albert about an experience he had in another foxhole, a couple of months earlier. They were pinned down by heavy enemy fire. He was scared to death, but the other guy was calm and not scared at all. The other guy talked about how Jesus was his Savior and he didn't have to be afraid. He told him that time was short. Many of the soldiers would not survive the war and Eddy could be one of them. He warned Eddy that if he died without Christ, he would be forever doomed. His testimony was so compelling that Eddy believed him. The guy prayed with him and Eddy said that a mysterious, but calming, perfect peace came over him, and he was no longer afraid to die.

Albert often wondered about Eddy's peace. He saw it on Eddy's face in his last battle. Eddy fearlessly fought his way up the hill, being the first to reach the enemy bunkers, he pitched a grenade into the bunker, making it possible for the American forces to advance. His heroic exploits continued, until eventually, he was caught between enemy artillery fire and the American tanks. Eddy's body was violently torn apart by a German 88mm anti-tank weapon. The horrible image of Eddy's death was forever etched into Albert's mind that some days brought a mournful sadness that was hard to shake. That was a day he wished he had never seen, a day he wished he could forget; but the memory was as fresh as ever.

Chapter 11

Buck lazily plodded across the hay field in front of Mr. Roy's house. Charlie rode bareback holding a piece of leftover well rope that was coiled into a lasso. Elly Mae followed close beside the horse, but leery of the rope. Ahead, Charlie spotted a lone pine sapling, that stood about four feet tall, in the middle of the hay field. He straightened his posture, gathered his rope into a loop, and kicked Buck in the sides with both heals. Charlie imagined the sapling to be a calf, and he was going to rope it. Buck, in blind obedience, guided by the reigns, and urged on by two blunt heels in the ribcage, sped toward the sapling. Charlie eyed his target with determined focus, as he swung the giant loop. Approaching the innocent little sapling, Charlie flung the loop and caught the tree. He was pleasantly surprised that it was captured in just one try, until he realized that the rope was tangled around his hand, and Buck was running full speed past the tree with no inclination to stop!

Although it happened too quickly to respond; it also seemed like time stood still. In slow motion, he could see the speeding horse, the noose tightening on the tree, and the slack going out of the rope. He even had time to think about the outcome of the situation, and how stupid he was. Then abruptly, the sense of slow motion ended, and real time returned. Big, scared, overstretched eyes, and tight lips described Charlie's face when he realized that things were about to get very ugly! The rope reached the end of its capacity, and so did Charlie's arm, bringing his inertia to a sudden and immediate stop. During the brief time that he hung in mid air, Charlie observed the bottom of Buck's rear hooves as he sped away, up the hill, throwing dirt and grass into his distorted face. He wondered if Buck might be thinking, that this was all part of the plan. But Charlie had no plan. He never had a plan. He never thought through any scenario before acting. To be honest, Charlie's roping skills were pretty pitiful, and he didn't expect to actually catch the tree.

He lay stretched out on the ground with one arm tied to the sapling and extended like Superman when he was about to launch into outer space. That's when Elly Mae came along and inserted her cold nose into his ear, giving him a wet willy. Surprised to still be alive, he rolled over onto his back and lay there groaning while removing the tangled rope from his wrist. The whole time, Elly Mae excitedly licked his face and neck until he finally scrambled to his feet.

Charlie sheepishly looked around hoping no one saw the embarrassing exploit. But Mr. Roy was already on the floor of his front porch rolling with laughter. He had seen the whole thing. Charlie came strolling up to Mr. Roy leading Buck with his head hung down and shoulders slumped. Mr. Roy was leaning against a post and drinking a beer.

"Hey cowboy! That was some fancy roping!" He bent over, slapped his knee and laughed, as he continued, "You're lucky that tree didn't run away and drag you across the creek!" Charlie could only blush and take the ribbing as Mr. Roy dished it out. However, when the jokes ended, Mr. Roy became serious and said, "You know that you could have been hurt real bad pulling that stunt?" Charlie answered, "Yes Sir, I know now." Feeling a little fatherly, Roy continued, "If you are going to be a real cowboy, you will need a saddle. I've got one in the barn that you can have, if you want it? You'll have to clean and oil it, but it's a good saddle." Charlie's countenance brightened and a smile spread across his face.

After a couple more beers and some elbow grease, Roy and Charlie had that saddle looking like new. "Ole Buck looked good with that saddle cinched on him," Charlie thought as he was leaving the barn. Again feeling fatherly, Mr. Roy jovially removed his cowboy hat and handed it to Charlie. "Here son. You can fold some paper and put it under the sweat band to make it fit." Charlie's grin was wider than the grill on his daddy's truck. "Wow! Thanks Mr. Roy! What do I owe you for all of this stuff?" Mr. Roy laughingly popped off, "You can repay me by not roping any more trees."

Charlie sat high in his new saddle, wearing his too big hat that folded his ears down as it covered his eyebrows and half of his eyes. But he could still see Mr. Stokes stagger past him on the path to Mr. Roy's house.

In slurred speech and misdirected pointing Mr. Stokes said, "Coww-bouy! Did yoou leave some—for me?" He was referring to Mr. Roy's place and Mr. Roy's bottle. Mr. Stokes always came to Mr. Roy's when he ran out of whiskey and money. Roy obliged him because he was lonesome and didn't like to drink alone. Usually before the day was over, they were both stumbling drunk and sometimes they both passed out.

Alcohol affected Roy in a comical and generous way, but Mr. Stokes usually turned mean. The two men were on the ground wrestling when Miss Rhody walked up carrying a fistful of freshly picked flowers. She kicked them both with the side of her shoe several times, until finally they became aware of her presence.

"Roy! You ought to be ashamed of yourself! Out here acting like a fool! - Stokes you git on home and don't show your face around here again!" Stokes didn't argue. He just got up from the ground and stumbled away. He didn't want to mess with Miss Rhody. He knew she was one of them holy rollers and she would put the fear of God in ya.

After Stokes left, Miss Rhody tore into Roy, "I come out here to put flowers on momma's grave and what do I find you doing?.... My little, old man of a brother, is brawling on the ground like a teenager! When are you going to grow up? You would think sixty eight years old would be old enough! You act more like daddy everyday! He's the reason poor momma was put into an early grave.... And what is that drunkard, Stokes doing over here? What were you two fighting about anyway?" Roy smiled and slurred at her, "I told him that he was uglier than me! And that's when he jumped on me! I was only defending myself!"

Miss Rhody unamused by his answer, ranted on, "Did I see Charlie Pickle come from down here earlier? You better not be drinking and acting like a fool around that boy! Don't you corrupt him like daddy corrupted you!"

On that comment Roy hung his head in shame. That's why he never married and had children. He didn't want anybody to be like him.

Chapter 12

"Buuudeeee....Eeeennaaaa....!!!" Lizzie yelled with her hands cupped around her mouth like a megaphone. Her children's names being stretched so they would echo down through the hollow. Charlie and Enna were in the creek hunting salamanders. Charlie told her, "That's momma calling us." Lizzie called again, "Buuudeeee....Eeeeennaaaa!!!!"

Around Misty Hollow, it was common to hear mommas call for their children in this manner. Everybody knew that if momma called, you better be in earshot, and you better "git home."

Buck was tied to a bush near the creek. Charlie urgently led him down into the creek and jumped onto the saddle from the tall bank. Enna and Elly Mae scurried up the hill with Charlie coming behind. Charlie was swinging a well rope over his head, like a lasso, when His momma yelled again, "Buuuudeeee.... Eeeennaaaa....!!! Charlie yelled back, "Maaa'aaam?" "Ya'll come here!" She yelled.

When they both arrived at the fence, she told them, "Go over to Miss Rhody's and borrow her ice cream freezer." Enna piped in, "Momma, can I take the wagon?" She was referring to her brother's Red Flyer. Lizzie responded, "That's a good idea Enna. You can haul the freezer back and not have to carry it by hand!"

Enna struck out pulling the little wagon, and Charlie followed behind her swinging the well rope over his head. As Lizzie watched them leave, an after thought entered her mind and she yelled, "Buddy, don't you tie that rope to that wagon!" Charlie replied, with obedience in his tone, "Yes ma'am."

Miss Rhody graciously handed the freezer to Charlie and watched him place it in the wagon. She said, "Now Charlie, take care of my freezer!"

After agreeing to take good care of the freezer and thanking Miss Rhody, Enna grasped the handle and headed up the road. The wagon had big wheels which made it easy for Enna to pull; but, Charlie thought it would be much easier if Enna got inside the wagon and let Buck do the pulling. Enna said, "Momma told you not to tie Buck to the wagon!" Charlie replied, "She won't know! Get in the wagon!" Enna got into the wagon, hugging the freezer with both arms and legs, while Charlie tied the rope to the saddle and then to the wagon tongue. Charlie climbed aboard the horse and bumped his ribcage with the heals of his bare feet. The wagon began to rattle, and Buck became frightened by the strange squeaking sounds. His gait gradually increased as he stepped sideways attempting to see the source of the squeaking and clattering noise behind him. He ran faster and faster trying to escape, but the contraption kept pace with him. Once Buck realized that the scary wagon was chasing him, he ran away, out of control. Charlie knew he had messed up again when he could not stop the horse. The faster Buck ran, the louder the wagon rattled. Charlie looked back at Enna and she was holding on for dear life, still hugging the freezer. The expression on her face revealed her terror. Charlie pulled on the reigns and yelled, "Whoa Buck!" But the horse ignored his attempts and sped faster down the dirt road.

Charlie looked behind him again. Enna still sat in the wagon hugging the freezer with the same look of frozen terror on her face, but this time, the whole rig was airborne and flying like a wingless airplane. He looked forward and pulled on the reigns again, desperately yelling at the top of his lungs, "Whoa Buck!!!" They were coming near to the house, and the horse was still out of control. He jumped the road ditch and ran through the yard until he reached the front porch, where he came to a bouncing stop.

Lizzie saw the run away horse pulling something behind it from the kitchen window. She instantly ran onto the porch and with a seriously distressed expression asked Charlie, "Where's your sister?"

Charlie's head snapped around expecting to see his sister behind him, but there was only a rusty tongue lying on the ground, vainly being held secure by the double knot he had tied with the frayed, well rope. Charlie thought about Enna and the wagon flying in the air towards him and quickly responded to his mother's question, "I don't know! Last time I seen her, she was headed this a way!"

After giving Charlie a very disapproving look, she pounced off of the porch and ran down the road frantically looking for Enna. A few hundred yards around the curve, she saw Enna in a crumpled pile against a gum tree. Elly Mae was already there. She nudged the baby with her nose then ran to Lizzie and then back to the baby. Blood streamed from Enna's little head, and she was unconscious.

The tongueless wagon lay upside down in the ditch. The broken freezer lay strewn about Enna's crumpled body. Lizzie scooped her daughter up from the ground and sprinted back towards home. She met Charlie on the way and screamed, "Go to the the field and get your father!" Charlie kicked Buck in the ribs, and the horse galloped into the bottom where Albert was plowing.

Lizzie brought Enna into her bedroom and began cleaning the wound on her head. She called her name while crying profusely, "Enna? Enna? Wake up baby! Wake up sweetheart! Enna? Enna? You're home now honey! Wake up sweetie!"

Enna never stirred; her body remained limp, and her face was void of any expression. The wound on Enna's temple was gaping and still bleeding. Lizzie held pressure on the wound to stop the bleeding while crying and talking to her. Albert and Charlie came running into the bedroom. Albert yelled frantically, "How is she?" The frightful expression on Lizzie's face told Albert all he needed to know. He gently cradled his daughter in his arms and carried her to the truck. Lizzie and Charlie followed and were in the truck, at the same time, as Albert and Enna. Albert raced to the infirmary praying that his daughter would make it.

Upon arrival, the staff moved with a sense of urgency, recognizing the seriousness of Enna's injuries. During the doctor's examination, she lay almost lifeless on the gurney where Albert stood holding her hand.

Finally, she stirred slightly, and Albert's heart jumped. She opened her muddled eyes and foggily said, "Where are we? Where's momma? Where's Charlie?" Enna raised a feeble hand to touch her throbbing temple. The nurse was working there to clean the wound. Finding wet blood, Enna panicked. She had never seen her own blood before. Confusion, combined with fear, welled up into crying and screaming. Lizzie cradled her little body near, "It's alright Baby, You're going to be okay."

After cleaning the blood and stitching her temple, the doctor informed Albert and Lizzie that Enna suffered from a severe concussion. There was a possibility that there could be dangerous after effects in the future. His greatest concern though was her welfare right now. He did not know if there were internal injuries or not. It would be best if she were kept at the infirmary for a few days, for observation.

Lizzie remained with Enna, while Albert and Charlie went home. On the way home from the infirmary, Albert and Charlie were quiet. Both were thinking about Enna; both were terribly concerned.

Over the next few days, Albert learned all the details about what had happened. Enna told her side of the story. Miss Rhody, glad that Enna was doing better, told everyone not to worry about that old freezer. However, Charlie's day of reckoning came in the form of a stern scolding from his father.

Albert began his tirade, "Your mother told me what happened. She told you not to tie the wagon to the horse. Instead, you did it anyway. Your sister is severely injured, she could have died! As a matter of fact, she's not out of danger yet! The doctor is concerned about the possibility of residual complications from this. You have been spending way too much time with Mr. Hoots. You're starting to act like him. His name has always been a topic for gossip and ridicule. He also has a reputation for being careless, especially for those closest to him. He doesn't take anything seriously, and everything is a joke. He drinks like a sailor! Is that the kind of person you want to grow into?" Albert never gave Charlie the opportunity to answer that question before continuing, "Your mother said that you made some comical remark when she asked you about your sister? Everything is not funny! Sometimes you have to be serious; and, all the time, you have to be careful with other people's lives! Your mother and I will not tolerate disobedience!" Albert continued his tirade: "Miss Rhody asked you to take care of her freezer! Instead, you had no consideration for her property, and you busted it to pieces! You will work for Miss Rhody, in her garden for the rest of the summer, until you pay her back for her freezer! That means you will not be hanging around Roy Hoots!....And furthermore, you get yourself braced for a good hide tanning!"

The next day, Charlie walked the short distance down the dirt road to Miss. Rhody's. On his way, he ruminated over the spanking that he knew was justified and the words of his father concerning Enna, "She could have died!—She's not out of danger yet!—There could be residual complications!"

He loved his sister and felt the most tender sorrow and remorse, hoping that nothing bad happened to her as a result of his stupidity.

He reported to Miss Rhody and told her he was sorry for breaking the ice cream freezer. Miss Rhody hugged him close and said, "That's alright Charlie. I can get another one. I just pray your sister fully recovers."

Miss Rhody didn't treat Charlie like a farm hand. She never made him feel like he was paying a debt or being punished. The work was shared, but Miss Rhody carried the heaviest burden. She made the work fun by telling Charlie a different joke every day. Soon, that turned into who could tell the funniest joke. Every task became a competition like: who could pick the most peas, or who could hoe their row the fastest, or who could find the most cucumbers on one vine. Also, Miss Rhody was the best cook in Misty Hollow. The longer Charlie worked for her, the bigger and stronger he grew. He wasn't fat; he was just well fed.

By the end of the summer, Charlie and Miss Rhody had become closer than ever. Charlie loved her like a grandmother. He asked her one day as they were shucking corn, "Miss Rhody? Would it be okay if I call you grandma Rhody?" Blushing with excitement and pride, she stood up and dumped a whole lap full of roasting ears in the dirt. She grabbed Charlie by surprise and gave him a momma bear hug while exclaiming, "Charlie! Nothing would make me prouder! I never had my own children even though I always wanted them. When I was still young, God sent me your mother to raise. I love her like a daughter, and I have always loved you and Enna like my own grandchildren!"

Back in the day, Stanley and Miss Rhody prayed for Rosemond Stuckey's little family. They grew a strong attachment to Lizzie who opened her heart to them ever since she was a little girl. Perhaps, it was because she carried such a heavy burden and needed a mother to replace the one she lost. However, her brothers were never close like that. When they reached adulthood, they went back to logging with their family in Eutaw Alabama. So far, they had not shown any interest in returning, not even to visit Lizzie and her family.

Chapter 13

Roy stood at the door humbly and reverently holding his hat by the curled brim with both hands. He gently called through the screen door, "Is anybody home?" He didn't want to disturb Enna if she was resting. Lizzie came out of the back room and greeted him, "Hello, Mr. Hoots. How have you been?" He responded, "I've been doing fine. I heard about your daughter's accident and I just came by to see how she was doing? Lizzie opened the door and stepped into the breezeway with Mr. Hoots. She pointed at a rocking chair and said, "Please, sit down. Can I get you some ice tea?" He replied, while wiping beer sweat from his forehead, "You sure can. This summer heat is terrible."

Lizzie fetched him and herself a cold glass of tea, and they sat in the breezeway talking about the children and the accident. She told him all that the doctor had said and about how Charlie was being punished. She also thanked him for giving Charlie the saddle and cowboy hat which had become his most valued possessions. Lizzie expressed to Mr. Hoots how grateful she was for taking Charlie under his wing while Albert was away. He needed a man's influence in his life at that time so badly.

Just then, a surprised Albert stepped up onto the porch. "Howdy Mr. Hoots." Roy stood up to shake Albert's hand, "How are you, Albert?" He responded, "I'm fine. My fields are all looking real good. I hope to have a bumper crop this year." Lizzie interjected, "Mr. Hoots came by to check on Enna—Albert, sit down and let me get you a cold glass of tea before supper." Albert sat down and Lizzie disappeared into the house for tea.

Roy spoke, "Albert, I'm very sorry for what has happened to your little girl. I hope she will be okay. Charlie was coming by to visit me every now and then, but Lizzie said he was working off a debt at Rhody's as part of his punishment." Roy continued, "Charlie is a fine young man. He has a heart as big as Texas, and boy, that sense of humor is something else. I remember the first time I met him. He showed up over there at my place one day when I was putting up winter hay. I was busy stacking hay around the pole when I heard a little voice shout, "Hey mister, it would be easier to bury that pole if you would lay it down!"

Albert and Roy laughed. Then Albert said, "That boy has a "matter of fact" way of looking at things; and somehow, it always comes out funny."

Then Albert confessed to Roy, "I reckon I should tell you, part of Charlie's punishment included no more visits to your house. Don't get me wrong, I know that you have been good to Charlie, but I'm concerned about your influence in other ways. Charlie has never been around alcohol, and I don't want him to think that it's okay or acceptable."

Roy replied seriously, "Albert, I can see where this would concern you. My daddy drank too much, and I unintentionally patterned my life after his. It wasn't something I set out to do; it just ended up that way. It's all I ever knew. But since Charlie started coming around, I see the goodness in him that I never had. I can tell that he has been raised by good people." Roy continued, "If you will let the boy come visit, I will stop drinking around him. I don't want him to live the kind of life that I have lived. I know that a boy needs discipline. It's good to have a daddy that cares enough to do it with love. My daddy never had any love in him. He had nothing but hate until the day he died."

Lizzie returned with Albert's tea and asked, "Mr Hoots, can I get you a refill?" Roy replied, "No thank you, Lizzie. I've got cows to milk. I better be going!" Lizzie responded, "You'll have to come for supper sometime." Roy replied, "I'd be delighted. An old bachelor like me don't get much home cooking." Then Roy respectfully looked to Albert and said, "Albert, I promise I will do right by Charlie, if you will please reconsider and let him come for visits." Albert graciously responded, "Roy, I can see that you mean what you say. Any man can change, and I believe you. But, Lizzie and I will have to talk about it." Roy bowed his head to Lizzie out of respect and said, "Thank y'all, and I'll see you later."

Finally, the summer was almost over and Charlie's punishment was complete. Also, by the end of summer, Enna was fully recovered and doing well.

One morning at breakfast, Albert told Charlie that it would be alright for him to go and visit his old friend, Mr. Roy; but, if there was any drinking or misbehaving, he was to come home immediately. The news made Charlie happy, and he excitedly began making plans to go that morning to visit Mr. Roy. Lizzie interjected, "You're not going anywhere today. You and Enna have six rows of purple hull peas to pick, and there will be no playing until they are picked and shelled."

Charlie's head dropped as he shuffled off to the garden. He was tired of the garden. Especially since that was all he had been doing all summer. Enna soon joined him. Charlie didn't want to work, but he knew his momma would tan his hide if he didn't do what she told him to do.

He and Enna picked peas for about ten minutes until the wad of marbles in his front pocket got his attention. Apparently, Mr. Stanley Fletcher and his siblings played a lot of marbles. Charlie picked them up in grandma Rhody's garden and collected them all summer.

He asked Enna excitedly, "You want to play marbles?" Enna nodded indicating that she would like to play. Charlie drew a circle in the dirt and showed her how to play. He bragged, "Grandma Rhody taught me how to play marbles." Enna asked, "Why do you call Miss Rhody "grandma"?" Charlie responded, "Cause she loves me like her own grandson." Enna asked another question, "Would she care if I called her "grandma"?" Charlie replied matter of factly, "Naw, she loves you that way too."

After Charlie and Enna had played away an hour or so, their momma yelled from the back porch, "Are y'all finished picking those peas?" Charlie paused briefly to contrive an answer, then yelled, "All we like, is finishing up." Lizzie smiled and shook her head while speaking to herself, "That boy will never change. At least, I hope he doesn't."

Chapter 14

"Wow! A double barrel shotgun!" Charlie saw the youth size shotgun with a red bow tied to it, the card read, "Merry Christmas to my pal Charlie, from Santa!" "Wow! How did he know I wanted a shot gun? Look daddy! Santa brought me a shotgun! Now I can go squirrel hunting with you down in *The Hardwoods*!"

Albert loved Charlie's excitement. It reminded him of his own childhood at Christmas time. Each year his father grew a long beard and dressed up like Santa Claus to fool the kids. They sang fun songs like *Jingle Bells* and *Jolly Old Saint Nick*.

The stockings were nothing fancy, just old socks stretched out of proportion by the oranges and pecans that were stuffed into them. His mother always loved leading the children as she sang, *Away in the Manger*, and talked to them about Jesus being born on Christmas. But Santa was more fun and exciting to Albert, so those were the traditions he was handing down to his own children.

Everyone's attention on Charlie's shotgun was diverted by a strange noise coming from behind the Christmas tree. Something was back there moving around.

"Baaaaa! Baaaaa!"

Lizzie asked Enna, "What's making that strange sound?" She continued, "Go see what it is."

Enna pulled a limb back on the tree to reveal a slatted wooden crate, "Baaaa! Baaaa!" Startled, Enna let go of the limb and stepped back. "Go see what it is. What does that card say on the side?" Lizzie said, as she reached for the card and read it to Enna. "Merry Christmas to Enna who is as sweet and innocent as this little lamb! Love Santa." Enna ran to the crate and drug it from behind the tree. "Awwww!...Awww! She is so beautiful! My very own real lamb! Look daddy!Santa Claus brought me a real lamb!" Albert said, "I see! What are you going to name it?" Enna placed her index finger on her chin and studied a second. Then she said, "Clara!" Just like my wooden lamb!" Albert cut her short, "Sorry honey, "she" is a "he." You'll have to pick another name."

"Baaa! Baaa! Baaa! Baaa!" "Then I will call him Max."

"I think Max is hungry," Lizzie said as she went into the kitchen to fetch the bottle of milk that had been specially prepared for that moment. She returned to find Max standing in Enna's lap.

"Baaa! Baaa! Baaa!" Lizzie said, "Here, give him some milk, and he will stop crying" while handing Enna the bottle. Enna offered the nipple to the lamb who had searched desperately for ninny on her arm. After receiving the nipple and lunging at it as if nursing his momma, the bottle was emptied in minutes. Max made a new best friend, and Enna had someone to talk to besides her dolls.

The next morning, Albert and Charlie went into *The Hardwoods* squirrel hunting. Charlie had never gone squirrel hunting with his own shotgun before.
Albert taught him how to load and carry the gun. He told him, "This gun is not a toy. It is a tool that is used to harvest meat for the table. It is deadly to animals and humans. Never point it at anyone. Always carry it with the barrel pointing up or down. Always leave the safety on until you are ready to pull the trigger. And always treat it like it is loaded, especially when you are cleaning it!"
After gun safety instructions, it was now time for Charlie to learn all about squirrel hunting, us-

ing the special *Albert Pickle Technique* that his father facetiously bragged about.

Charlie was excited and curious about the special hunting technique his father was about to teach him. After venturing deep into the woods, they sat near a hickory tree where Albert instructed him to be very still and quiet.

Soon there was movement in the trees above them. A squirrel jumped from a nearby sapling into the hickory tree. Albert stood up to shoot at the squirrel, but when the squirrel spotted him, it ran to the opposite side of the tree. Albert whispered to Charlie while pointing,

"Son, go around to the other side and shoot the squirrel!" As soon as Charlie walked around the tree, the squirrel came back to Albert's side and Albert shot him.

Charlie said disappointingly, "Awe! He moved!" Albert sheepishly grinned and picked up the squirrel. He then whispered to Charlie, "Come here and sit down. We'll wait on another one." Soon they heard squirrel claws scratching the bark as another one scurried up the tree. Albert stood to shoot at the squirrel, and it moved out of sight behind the tree. Albert again sent Charlie around to shoot it. The squirrel came back to Albert's side of the tree and he shot it.

Charlie redundantly remarked, "Awe! He moved again!" After the fourth exact episode, Charlie began to wise up to his father's trick! It wasn't long before another Squirrel scurried across the tree tops and came down in front of them. Albert stood up and the squirrel ran to the other side and Charlie stood up too but with a large stick in his hand as if he were going around the tree. Instead he pitched the stick into the bushes on the other side of the tree, spooking the squirrel, causing it to scurry back to Charlie's side where he was waiting with his shotgun raised and aiming. Blam!

He killed the squirrel and it fell at his feet. Albert then sheepishly said, "Well, not only have you learned the *Albert Pickle Technique* of squirrel hunting, you have even perfected it!"

After the squirrel hunt, Albert suggested a walk along the fence row which bordered the creek bank. This is where where the broom sage and blackberry briars became habitat for cane cutter rabbits.

The time Albert spent fighting in Europe honed his mental awareness of all surroundings. He was able to keenly spot irregularities in the foliage and landscape. Looking down the fence a hundred yards, he saw the top strand of barbed wire pulled tightly downward and the dormant vegetation in front of it was cleared away for a space of about four feet. It appeared there was something large entangled in the fence. As they cautiously approached the spot, Albert recognized a white tailed deer. He hadn't seen many deer in his lifetime and Charlie had never seen a one.

Deer were scarce in Mississippi. They were almost decimated during the Civil War and hardly recovered by the 1920's. Night time rabbit hunters thinned them down to almost zero during the Great Depression because everyone was hungry. If not for relocation of the species from Mexico and North Carolina, they may have gone extinct in the whole state.

He pointed at the deer and said to Charlie, "Shhhh" while holding his index finger vertically across his puckered lips. He wasn't sure if the deer was still living, and if it was, he didn't want to cause any unnecessary stress to the animal.

Albert's closer inspection revealed that the small framed buck had been there too long and was nearly dead. He was surprised that the buzzards had not already killed him because all of the fight was gone out of him, and his eyes were glazed.

It was illegal to kill a whitetail deer in Mississippi, but he was not about to let the animal suffer any longer. He pulled his pistol from its holster and a single shot, point blank, behind the ear ended its misery.

The little buck possessed two inch spiked antlers which Albert saved just for novelty. He tossed them in the root cellar where the scalp dried up and fell off.

The next summer while playing in the root cellar, Charlie rediscovered the antlers. They looked dusty and old after laying in the dirt all that time. He picked them up. As he inspected them closer, he realized that the antlers looked a lot like what he imagined the devils horns looked like.

Mischievous thoughts gathered in his mind. He began to formulate a plan to frighten Enna. With his mother's butter knife, he carved a neat, square cubbyhole in the dirt wall of the root cellar. He then situated the horns in the cubbyhole as if they were being stored there. Later, he found Enna playing under the shade tree with her dolls as Max peacefully chewed his cud.

"You want me to show you where the devil keeps his horns?" Charlie asked impishly. "You don't know where the devil keeps his horns," Enna stated plainly. Charlie retorted, "Yes I do. I can show you." Enna stood up and said, "Show me!"

He led her and Max around the house to the root cellar. He pulled the creaking door open. They stepped down into the dark, musty cellar. Charlie led Enna by the hand over to the dark corner where the horns were neatly placed in the cubbyhole: "See!—Look over there!"

Enna squinted and scanned the dark corner where Charlie was pointing. Sure enough, about face high to Charlie, she could see the horns neatly placed inside the square cubbyhole. A feeling of apprehension welled up inside her as Charlie began to explain about the horns. "Last summer when I was working at Grandma Rhody's, she told me about the devil. She said that he roams all over the earth, and he is like a roaring lion seeking someone to devour."

Enna stepped out of the darkness and into the doorway where she felt safer. Charlie, seeing that his sinister plan was working, continued, "This must be the place he stores his horns! He don't need them unless he is about to devour somebody! If you ever look in here and there're gone, then you will know that he has been here and somebody has been devoured!" Enna was terrified and fled from the cellar with Max bumping her leg closely as he ran along beside of her.

That night Enna dreamed that the devil came to get his horns from the root cellar. He produced an evil moaning sound as he reached for his horns and placed them on his ugly head: "Uhhhmmm!!!....Uhhmmm!!!"

She awoke suddenly, her heart pounding with fear. It was only a dream. She snuggled Max a little closer, listening and hearing nothing, she relaxed a little and closed her eyes for sleep.

"Uhhmmm!!!....Uhhmmm!!!" Enna jolted fully awake and sprung upright. She strained to hear the sound again. Was the dream real? Was the devil coming to get his horns?

The full moon cast shadows across her bedroom. And then faintly, in the distance, she heard the devil's moan again and it seemed to be advancing towards the house!
"Uhhmmm!!!....Uhhmmm!!!....
Uhhmmm!!!....Uhhmmm!!!"

Enna crawled from her bed and crept to the window which faced the *Hardwoods*. She could see a bright figure in the edge of the trees, half stumbling, half crawling, maybe floating. Having movements like a ghost, the mysterious being slowly ascended the hill, along the footpath, leading from the spring. The ghoulish moan grew louder and more pronounced as it came closer and closer. "Uhhmmm!!!.....Uhhmmm!!!"

Enna ran to her bed and dove under the covers. Her heart was filled with dread of the creature as it approached the house.
"Uhhmmm!!!....Uhhmmm!" Enna peeked from under the covers!

Oh no! There it was looking into the window. Its dark, circled eyes roamed from side to side as they searched fearlessly around her bedroom. The creature's pale complexion was accented by the glowing moon. Its sunken cheeks were so deep, they produced shadows. Its pointed nose and chin protruded past long, stringy hair.

The creature's persistent moaning grew louder as it scratched the window pane with its long fingernails and then boldly began beating on the window with two flat palms demanding entrance into her bedroom. "Uhhmmm!!!....Uhhmmm!!!"

Enna trembled with terror, but poked her head from under the cover long enough to let out a blood curdling scream. The creature scowled in response as if encouraged by her screams. Its pounding on the window grew loader and more forceful. Enna screamed louder and more frantically. This time, she called for the only one she knew of who could save her, "Daa-ddy!!!Daa-ddy!!!"

Albert came tearing into the room stumbling from sleep and the darkness. "What's wrong Enna?" She flew out of the bed and into her father's embrace, "Daddy, there's a witch outside my window!" Lizzie came into the room holding a lantern just as the creature beat on the window and moaned, "Uhhmmm!!!....Uhhmmm!!!" She drew near to her husband and shakily asked, "What is it Albert?" Albert did not respond to her question because he had no answer. While holding his daughter and Lizzie holding him, they backed out of the room in one terrified unit. Lizzie hardly noticed Max leaning tightly against her knees.

They closed the bedroom door to create a barrier between them and the creature. As Albert handed Enna over to Lizzie, he eased past the fireplace and picked up a piece of firewood. He cautiously descended the front steps, clutching the fire wood in cocked position as a club.

It wasn't long before a relieved, but obviously concerned, Albert came walking around the house helping the creature up onto the porch. Lizzie and Enna peeked from the door and could hear muffled conversation. Albert was asking, "Is anything broken? Do you need a doctor?" Lizzie then recognized that it was Mrs. Stokes. She and her husband lived in a broken down shack, a half mile away, on the north ridge of Misty Hollow. She struggled every day because Mr. Stokes was an alcoholic. He would get in a drunken rage and act out violently towards her, but otherwise he was a coward.

Albert brought Mrs. Stokes into the house and offered her a seat on the sofa. She gathered her blood stained night gown from under her as she sat. Her naked feet were bleeding and dirty. Hollowed cheeks, pronounced by a slender face, and the absence of teeth, caused her wrinkled lips to pucker. Mr. Stokes had blackened both eyes and bloodied her nose. Her thin gray hair streamed from the crown of her head in a disheveled way.
Certainly, she looked like a witch. Enna had never been so afraid, but she felt sorry for Mrs. Stokes.

Because of the late hour, Lizzie insisted that Mrs. Stokes remain for the night. In the morning after breakfast, Albert could talk to Mr. Stokes. Perhaps, he would be sober by then and more reasonable to discuss matters.

The next morning Lizzie looked through her closet and brought Mrs. Stokes a clean yellow dress and a bonnet to cover her messy hair. Lizzie informed Mrs. Stokes that she would be in the barn milking the cows and would cook breakfast afterwards. However, Mrs. Stokes insisted that Lizzy allow her to cook breakfast since they have all been so kind to her. Lizzie consented and went on to the barn.

Charlie slept through the entire night and groggily arrived at the breakfast table oblivious to the whole episode. Sitting at his usual place between Enna and his father, he noticed his mother's yellow dress as she stood cooking at the stove with her back to the table. He didn't really understand why she was wearing a bonnet. She sometimes wore a bonnet while milking the cows, but never while cooking breakfast.

He barely noticed as she held the skillet full of freshly scrambled eggs before him and dished a serving into his plate.

She never said a word and Charlie didn't look up. He just sleepily shoveled the eggs into his mouth. Quietly, she placed the empty skillet on the stove top and sat down at the table across from Charlie.

There was the usual sound of utensils rattling against the plates, but no conversation.

Charlie lazily swallowed a fork full of eggs and reached for his glass of milk. As he turned the glass up, his eyes locked in mutual gaze with the ghoulish creature across the table wearing his momma's dress!

The sudden revelation was expressed by Charlie spewing his milk across the table while fleeing backwards in frightened terror. His chair flipped out from under him as he slammed his back into the wall.

Albert leapt up and profusely apologized while wiping milk from her face, "Mrs. Stokes! Are you okay? I'm so very sorry!—Charlie! What are you doing? Have you lost your mind?"
Max and Elly Mae licked milk from the floor as Enna wiped milk from the table. Charlie stammered in an attempt to explain, "Well! — I didn't know it was Mrs.Stokes! Where is Momma!? And why is Mrs. Stokes wearing her dress and bonnet!?" Albert demanded that Charlie apologize to Mrs. Stokes! Charlie came near and sincerely apologized to Mrs. Stokes. He didn't know any details of what had happened; but, he knew by the appearance of her bruised face that it had something to do with Mr Stokes and his drinking.

Chapter 15

The double barrel shotgun rested on Charlie's shoulder as he leisurely strolled down the trail, through the hollow, leading to Grandma Rhody's house.

The tall ferns brushed his legs along the narrow path. His bare feet pounded the smooth, moist dirt, packed by the high volume of traffic between their homesteads. Elly Mae faithfully trod along behind him, looking at his heals and lightly panti- ng.

With a quick glance ahead, Charlie detected something odd standing upright in the middle of the path. Coming closer, he realized it was a cottonmouth, exposing its pasty white palate and needle sharp fangs!

The nasty creature resembled a hungry bird eagerly waiting for its mother to drop a worm into it's mouth. It measured about two feet long and was as big around as a man's wrist. The scaly, gray stump of a snake was deadly and poised to strike. The venomous serpent stood like a sentry in the middle of the path as if to guard and prevent pas- sage.

Grandma Rhody always said, "Snakes are like the devil; either one will kill you if they get the

chance! If we don't bruise their head; they will
120

 bruise our heal." Charlie pointed the double barrel at the snake, removed the safety and
squeezed the trigger. "Blam!" "You ain't gonna
get a chance to bruise my heal, serpent!"
Then with Elly Mae's help and a stick, they ex-
amined the dead snake, being cautious of the
lethal fangs. Once they were satisfied that the
snake was dead, Charlie picked it up by its tail
and tossed it out of harms way, before continuing down the path to Grandma Rhody's house.
In the heavy timber, lying on the hillside, was a
hollow log belonging to a hive of honey bees.
Hav- ing never been threatened, they were
docile to- wards people. Charlie approached the
hive many times in the past, and they never offered to harm him.
On this day, Charlie felt a little more mischievous than usual. After all, he already had a cottonmouth under his belt. He looked at his shotgun and then at the bees. He thought to himself,
"Why not shoot the bees?" Charlie backed off a
safe distance from the log, anticipating the bees
reac- tion. He remembered the yellow-jackets he
en- countered the first time he went into the
woods by himself. He hadn't forgotten how per-

sistent and smart they were. However, he was sure these bees would probably just swarm around the log, because they looked dumber than Yellow-jackets; and besides, the last time he looked at one up

121

close, it didn't have any ears, so it wasn't possible for them to trace the sound of the blast back to him.

With the shotgun leveled at the hive, Charlie clicked the safety to the off position. He took care- ful aim at the tiny hole in the log where bees trav- eled to and from the hive. Just as his finger touched the trigger, a bee stung him in the back of the head! He dropped the shotgun and ran, ex- pecting more stings, but they never came. As he reached the crest of the hill, Grandma Rhody was on her knees petting Elly Mae and talking sweet to her. Upon looking up, she acknowledged him, "What you up to Charlie? I heard a gunshot in the hollow, figured it was you, but I don't guess it was, cause you ain't got no gun." Charlie rubbed his stinging head, not really knowing how to answer Grandma Rhody. "Well grandma, that was me shooting. I killed a cottonmouth in the hollow." Grandma Rhody curiously asked, "Where's your gun? Why are you rubbing your head?" Charlie responded with an indirect answer, "Grandma, bees are smart!"

During the confession of his ridiculous act, Grandma Rhody developed a grave look on her face and she reprimanded Charlie, "Now that's about the dumbest thing I ever heard come out of anybody's mouth in all my born days!" She con- tinued, "Don't you know what would have hap-

 pened if you had shot that hive? Those bees would have covered you up and stung you to death!" Charlie hung his head in shame and nod- ded in understanding and agreement. The look of self loathing on Charlie's face caused her to back down and to speak with a softer voice as she con- tinued, "That was a sentry bee that stung you and he saved your life. Bees are the smartest insects that ever graced God's green earth. I believe God knew what you were about to do and sent that bee to stop you! He must have something big planned for you Charlie Pickle, cause He saved you from two perils al- ready this morning: first, from the snake, and then from yourself!" And then without even taking a breath she said, "Let's walk down there and get your shotgun."

Her mention of how God had saved him, made Charlie remember last summer when he was sent to work for Grandma Rhody. Being assigned to her custody for the summer, he was captive to all her preaching and teaching as they worked and sweated together in that garden. She explained how in the beginning there were no weeds to pull. No one had sweat on their brow from toiling in the hot sun 'cause the sun wasn't hot. And there was no rain. A cool mist rose from the ground and watered the garden. God walked in the garden with His immortal children and every- thing was good. That's when Grandma Rhody

123

deeply sighed and exclaimed, "Disobedience changed all of that Charlie! Good was stolen from the earth by simple disobedience! God's children ignored what He told them because their own logic seemed to be wiser to them, than His! God already knew that disobedience flung open the doorway to every evil thing. His children had unknowingly up- set the apple cart. Men began to do what was right in their own eyes, rather than listening to God's perfect plan.

A curse was set in motion that day. God no longer dwelt with his children because of His nature that would not allow Him to be in the presence of evil. The whole earth groaned and was now cursed, bringing forth weeds, mildew, rot, death and destruction. His children were no longer immortal. Now, they were subject to the curse of death, which was new to them and something they had never seen before! The devil was there that day. He was the instigator! Good was stolen, and he was the thief that came to steal it! That's all he does; steal, kill and destroy! He murdered all of mankind by simple deception."

Chapter 16

"Son, let me tell ya! Back in the good-ole-days, we didn't have nothing to eat." Charlie sat there listening as Mr. Roy cracked jokes about how difficult life was during the Great Depression. "I'm telling you that if a rabbit ran across the road, there would be three men chasing it! — We all knew that times were getting better when we was going to town one day and a rabbit ran across the road in front of us and only one man was chasing it." Charlie chuckled and Mr. Roy continued, "Seriously, it got so bad that we didn't have nothing but poke and grit wine." Charlie interrupted, "What is poke and grit wine?" Mr. Roy grinned and delivered the punch line, "Oh, that was when we would poke our feet out from under the table, grit our teeth and whine cause we didn't have nothing to eat!" Charlie amusingly laughed.

Then Mr. Roy changed the subject, "Did I ever tell you about my cousin Hilliard Hoots? We called him Hilly for short." "No sir," said Charlie. Mr. Roy began his story: "Well, he was about twelve years older than me, so this happened when I was small, but I remember hearing the story. — Anyhow, Ole Hilliard was a Jim Dandy football player. He was strong as a ox and some folks said he was twice as smart. He received offers from them fancy colleges to go to school free, just for playing football. When the time came for them to issue football uniforms, Hilly brought his home for the weekend. The next morning, about daylight, he dressed out in the whole uniform and went running just for practice. He cradled a football under his arm and jumped fences just like he was battling his way through a defensive line. At the end of his daddy's corn field he jumped the fence and ran through the woods to the far road. Before he knew it, he was plum over in Lick Skillet. Them folks in Lick Skillet are peculiar and superstitious. They were secluded and had never seen a football game, much less a football player. Well, Hilly knew several of them boys over there from when he worked at the sawmill and thought he might look them up while he was in the neighborhood. He came through the woods, darting around trees as if they were defensive players, hopping over fences, toting that ball with that brown leather helmet on his head, and them broad, padded shoulders rocking back and forth. His big, 'ole, cleated shoes was slinging grass and leaves out behind him like a bull pawing the dirt. Finally, he saw a couple of boys that he recognized, so he began to show out a little. He became more aggressive and began to grunt and growl as he dodged a bush or jumped a fence. When he got closer, he growled louder; his jog turned into a dead sprint right towards those fellas. Them boys were struck with fear and started stepping backwards. One of them asked the other, "What is it? What is it?" The other one responded, "I don't know! I don't know!" Soon, they found themselves backed up against the garden fence. There wasn't anything left to do but run into the woods because the thing kept coming towards them, like a mean bull chasing a rodeo clown. Hilly was too tired and out of breath to catch up with them, so he gave up and went back the way he came.

The next week, there was a rumor floating around that a tall, stocky monster with a brown bubble head, carrying a big rock under its arm came up the lane and angrily chased two residents of Lick Skillet into the woods. They figured the big rock was some sort of weapon used to kill its prey because it was pointy on both ends. The strange creature finally gave up his pursuit of the two men and is still running loose somewhere out there in the woods. The people in Lick Skillet have been bolting their doors and keeping their children inside until it's caught."

Charlie and Mr. Roy fell on the ground laughing. When Mr. Roy saw that he was on a roll; he continued, "Way before all that happened cousin Hilly was courting a half-Cajun gal named Fancy Lebreax, down near McIntyre Scatters. She was a pretty thing. He came under her spell on account of her beauty. She lived in a shack with her daddy whose name was Jacinto Lebreax. When Jacinto was a young man, he met her momma in New Orleans where they married. He didn't realize at the time, that she was not a Louisiana girl; but because he loved her, they left Louisiana and settled in her old family cabin on McIntyre Scatters. They lived a wonderful life together and soon were expecting. However, Mrs. Lebreax died giving birth and was buried in her family's cemetery on the banks of McIntyre Scatters. Jacinto named his little girl "Fancy" because that was the first impression he had of her momma the day he met her.

Jacinto made his living the same way his Acadian ancestors did in Louisiana. The only difference was, he was on the east end of Leflore county hunting, trapping, and fishing in the swamps and sloughs around McIntyre Scatters.

One day he noticed a momma skunk with her dainty little paw caught between two button willow branches. She was surrounded by a brood of ten babies that continued to nurse on her until she had become very weak. A skunk ain't got no large threshold for pain so she just stayed there without the will to escape or pull herself free. He reached the button willow with a stick and pried those branches apart to release her, but she was too weak to care for herself and her babies. He decided to take them home to his daughter who loved anything wild and she raised that brood of ten female skunks just like she was their mom-ma.

Fancy, being courting age, caused great concern for Jacinto. But, because of the skunks, he didn't have to worry about boys coming around; and besides, the skunks were jealous for her affection. Anytime someone came near her, the skunks backed up to them and raised their tails! However, being around them so much, Fancy got used to the smell and didn't notice it. That's when Hilly came along. Fancy was so pretty that he didn't seem to mind the smell, and the skunks didn't seem to mind him either. Those skunks took up with him just like they did with Fancy. Everywhere those two went, the skunks were right behind them. But, there came times when they wanted to go places that skunks weren't allowed. They tried putting them in a cage, but the skunks caused too big of a ruckus.

Now, I've heard that a skunk is kin to a cat. But I ain't never seen one in a tree or heard one purr. Anyhow, they love mice. So, anytime Hilly and Fancy wanted to go someplace that skunks were not allowed, they just led them down to the barn and when the skunks became occupied hunting mice under the crib, they snuck off and left them there.

Who knew there was a male skunk under the crib already? It wasn't long before Fancy had ten potbellied momma skunks following her around. When time came for them girls to have their kittens, they all went under Jacinto's shack and dug ten separate dens to raise their young. Within two months, they had over a hundred skunks living under the shack. Within two more months, it sounded like a wildlife play ground through the floor. By the end of the year, all the females were in heat and the males were rowdy and fighting. The whole place stunk so bad that it would burn your eyes just to walk down the road.

Jacinto wanted to capture the whole lot and take them far away into the next county, but Fancy just couldn't bring herself to part with them. So, Jacinto decided to move out of the shack and let the blasted skunks have it. He and Fancy moved into an abandoned fishing cabin on Tippo Run. He told his daughter, Fancy, that there never would be another petting critter of any kind brought to his house!"

After Fancy lost her brood of skunks and they moved to Tippo, Hilly's affections for Fancy became really serious and he began to stay at their house until late at night. Jacinto was weary of it and drove over to see Hilly's father about it. Hilly's father was my Uncle Hoot. I don't even know what his first name was, because everybody just called him Hoot. Anyway, Jacinto always mispronounced Hilly's given name. Hilly's mother gave him her grandfathers name because it had a distinguishing sound. When pronounced correctly it sounded like 'Hill-yird,' but, when Mr Lebreax said his name it sounded like 'Hilly-yard.' Jacinto spoke with a southern Cajun accent that sounded like this, "Mista Hoots, I like ya boy Hilly-yard. He's a good boy, but he comes to our house ever' day, and he stays too late. I cain't get no rest." Uncle Hoot told him, "Don't you worry about that any longer. I'll take care of it."

When Hilly got home late that night Uncle Hoot sheepishly asked Hilly, "Didn't Jacinto and Fancy move onto the west road at Tippo Run?"

Hilly responded, "Yes sir. They had to move on account of them skunks." Uncle Hoot continued, "The west road leading to Tippo Run is where that tragedy happened way back in 1820." Hilly asked, "What tragedy was that?" Uncle Hoot innocently continued while hanging his head, "Awww — it was sad. There was a wagon train of settlers going west. Back then the Mississippi delta was full of bears and as the train traveled along, a bear came out of the woods and mauled the team of horses on the lead wagon. That caused all the other horses to bolt and run through the woods leaving the wagons ripped up by the trees. They managed to kill the bear, but it was too late. The damage was done. Most of the people were dead; all the wagons were gone, but one.

They buried all the dead folks along the road facing the westward direction to commemorate their intended trek. The remainder of them loaded their belongings into the last wagon and continued on their journey."

Hilly dropped his head in disgust and said, "Man! That's terrible! That was a long time ago, but I feel bad for those folks."

Uncle Hoot continued as he sighed, "Yea, they say sometimes the bushes along the road start shaking for no reason — like the ghosts of those settlers are brushing past them, eternally walking west." There was an eerie sensation of hair standing up on the back of Hilly's neck as he hysterically responded, "Well, I don't believe in no ghosts!" Uncle Hoot calmly agreed, "Me either!"

The next day Hilly's skin was crawling off his body as he walked down that long west road to Tippo Run. He watched every bush thinking about those creepy ghosts eternally walking west. Uncle Hoot, unknown to Hilly, followed behind him later and tied long strings to several bushes. He then concealed the strings from sight and placed the other end where he could easily find them as they walked along the road.

The evening had turned dark by the time Uncle Hoot arrived at the Lebreax' cabin. He knocked on the screen door and was beckoned to come in. He explained how he had been planning to come visit and see their new cabin, but other things always kept him busy. Jacinto graciously invited him to supper where the conversation was centered mainly on the new cabin and the new opportunities for fishing and hunting around Tippo. Finally, Uncle Hoot looked at his watch and said, "My goodness! Look at the time! It has gotten late! It's a long walk in the dark and I better be getting on home." He arose to leave and Hilly did too. Undoubtedly, Uncle Hoot had put the scare into him pretty bad, and he wasn't about to walk home alone in the dark. He couldn't stand the idea of bumping shoulders with a ghost as they walked along the road; or stepping through their invisible bodies and feeling the cold chill of death!

Hilly walked at a brisk pace noticing every shadow cast by the full moon. Uncle Hoot was nearly out of breath from keeping such a fast gait, but he was still able to reach out and grab one of the strings, yanking it as they walked. Hilly spun around in the road and saw the bush shaking. Uncle Hoot gave it a couple more lite tugs just for the effects.

"Did you see that?" Hilly screeched. "Probably just a coon," Uncle Hoot consoled. They walked on. Uncle Hoot tried to strike up a conversation, but Hilly wasn't in the mood to talk. His nervous eyes rolled back and forth almost as if they could come out of their sockets and look behind him without turning his head. Uncle Hoot grabbed another string and tugged. The bush shook gently. They stopped in their tracks. He pulled the string again. While the bush was still shaking, Uncle Hoot found himself standing there all alone because Hilly was gone.

Uncle Hoot went back and gathered all his string before strolling on home with a big grin on his face. Hilly never did come home after dark again.

Mr. Roy's stories about Cousin Hilly intrigued Charlie and he asked, "What ever happened to your Cousin Hilly?" The expression on Mr. Roy's face turned non-comedic. With stammering speech, he tried to answer Charlie's question, "Uh — well — uhm — let's see — He married Fancy and they had a house full of kids; but, somewhere along the way, he got religion. Every time after that, when I saw him, he was spouting off about Jesus. I told him to stay away from me with all that junk! I didn't want to hear it! Uncle Hoot fell out with him too, because that's all he ever talked about. It was always, Jesus this, and Jesus that. Finally, Uncle Hoot told him, "If you don't have nothing else to talk about, just shut up!"

Everybody in the family started avoiding him. That is, except my sister Rhody. She didn't have enough sense to stay away, and before we knew it, she was a Holy Roller too! Then it spread to my momma. After all that happened, Hilly tried to convert my daddy, but daddy had better sense than to let Hilly get to him. He said, "Hilly wasn't nothing but a religious nut!" Rhody even converted Stanley before she would agree to marry him because she didn't want a husband like her daddy. I guess she would rather have a nut like herself.

Hilly and Fancy finally became too sophisticated for folks around here and moved to Tupelo. I lost touch with them, and don't know what happened after that; but, I bet them folks in Tupelo got tired of them too!

Charlie was surprised to hear Mr. Roy say that Grandma Rhody was his sister. Even though they lived fairly close to one another, he had never seen them together, or seen them act like family.

He loved Grandma Rhody because of the relationship that developed between them three summers before. She explained things in the Bible so he could understand them. The stories, from the Bible, that she told, always related to things that were happening in his own life. Jesus was always the main focus of every story. Grandma talked about how good Jesus was to her as if she knew him personally. Charlie could tell that Mr. Roy didn't care too much for Jesus, Grandma Rhody, or even Hilly. But that didn't matter because Charlie loved Mr. Roy anyway, since he and Mr. Roy had bonded early on.

Charlie often pondered about Jesus, the Bible, and Grandma Rhody's religion with a fair amount of interest. He even felt a sense of respect towards it all. But, he didn't understand why Mr. Roy's mood became dark with hatred when he heard Jesus' name.

Mr. Roy broke into his thoughts, "I hope you don't ever let those religious nuts turn you into a Hol...y Ro..ll ...." Mr. Roy's speech became slurred and broken right before his legs gave way, and he collapsed to the ground. His contorted face held the resemblance of a melted candle. His eyes reflected fear and confusion, but his vocal cords were unable to audibly report the cause of it all. In Charlie's wonderment and concern, he fell to his knees beside Mr. Roy and distressfully asked, "What's wrong?!"

Seeing that he was unable to respond, Charlie quickly ran for Mr. Roy's truck and drove near enough to access the passenger side door. Mr. Roy was very weak and uncoordinated, but Charlie was able to get him into the pickup.

Charlie climbed behind the wheel and crank the truck. He sped out of the yard, onto the dirt road that led past Grandma Rhody's house. Fortunately for Mr. Roy, Charlie was savvy to clutching and shifting because his father allowed him to drive the truck from town on occasion.

The excessive speed of the truck, coming in a cloud of dust, past Miss Rhody's house caused her to take notice. She recognized Roy's truck, but it was Charlie sitting in the drivers seat looking through the steering wheel. A sense of foreboding consumed her as the old truck dropped off of the hill leading to the one lane, wooden bridge just around a sharp curve. Charlie approached the curve at such great speed that he lost control. They were sideways by the time the pickup reached the old wooden bridge. The rear axle dropped off the edge and the truck skidded across on its rear frame to the other side. The speed of the truck and the force of the far bank against the rear end caused the truck to miraculously straighten in the center of the road. The whole dynamic occurred with such intensity that Charlie never removed his foot from the accelerator, which was pressed to the floor. They continued toward town in a thick cloud of dust that rendered the truck invisible to Miss Rhody's view. It appeared at first glance that Charlie ran off the bridge, but somehow she found solace after seeing the dense cloud of dust boil from behind the truck as it sped with ferocity up the hill towards town.

Miss Rhody did not know the circumstances, but was certain that something was very wrong with her little brother. She bounced up to Albert and Lizzie's house in Stanley's truck with the horn blasting wildly. They both bounded from the front steps in response to Miss Rhody's frantic alarm. She described the crisis in as few words as possible, prompting Albert to take the wheel from her as she slid over next to Lizzie who climbed into the passenger side. The speeding truck left a plume of dust all the way to the highway.

Upon arrival, they found Roy's truck abandoned on the grass at the front entrance of the infirmary. Roy lay on a gurney with doctors and nurses hovering while Charlie distraughtly observed from a close distance. When Charlie saw them enter the room, he rushed into their presence. They saw that he was visibly upset and Lizzie bent slightly to hug her half grown son. She spoke consolingly to him and gently inquired about the incident. Through tears, Charlie attempted to describe what he saw and what he did.

They were familiar with the symptoms that Charlie described. They had seen it before and its victims either died or were terribly maimed for the rest of their lives. Miss Rhody openly prayed, "Dear Lord, my little brother is separated from you. Preserve his life until the light of truth can pierce the darkness of his heart."

After a long wait, the doctor finally came to them with a full report of his condition. Roy was the victim of a massive stroke and if not for Charlie's quick response, he most likely would not have survived. However, he was still in danger and would need to remain in the infirmary for an undetermined period of time. The full extent of the damage was not yet known; but they should be able to tell within a few days, if he lived.

Buck's head dropped to the ground, burying his soft muzzle, nostril deep, into the manicured lawn. Charlie tethered him to a malleable low limb at the rear of the infirmary. He commanded Elly Mae to stay with Buck and she obediently laid down in the lush green grass.

As Charlie entered, he observed the beds lined up in perfect rows down the opposing walls of the large rectangular room. Each bed contained a pitiful soul dealing with a malady of their own. Some looked at Charlie as he passed, and others were unaware of his presence.

Mr. Roy's bed was the last one at the end of the room. As he approached, Charlie could see the right side of Mr. Roy's face was drawn down into a perpetual deep frown; but, the other side just looked sad, tired, and melted.

He walked up to Mr Roy's good side and sat down in a chair near the wall. Mr. Roy's eyes followed him, but he did not move or speak. The doctor met privately with Grandma Rhody and said that Roy could possibly regain the ability to shuffle along, but never to walk normally. His face would always be drawn, with no use of his right arm. He would probably never talk again; although, he would be able to comprehend speech.

Mr. Roy was unresponsive when Charlie greeted him. Charlie told him that he had ridden Buck to the infirmary, and that Buck and Elly Mae were in the back yard keeping each other company. He was also indifferent when Charlie shared the good news that he would be released in two days into Grandma Rhody's care. The one sided conversation soon ended when Charlie ran out of things to say. Reaching for Mr. Roy's good hand, he gave it a hefty shake and said, "I will be coming by Grandma Rhody's to see you." Mr. Roy's acknowledgement never came. Charlie carefully placed Mr. Roy's limp hand beside him and walked away. He thought about how Mr. Roy chose to live his life full of vigor, mixed with a little mischief. Most folks looked down on him for exhibiting those traits, but Charlie never saw any bad in him. He only saw a lonely old man offering kindness and friendship to a little boy whose only friends were a plug horse and a stray dog. Mr. Roy had been like a grandfather to Charlie, and he loved him for it.

Chapter 17

Enna rolled over, then sat upright in the dirt, where she found herself after being thrown by the spinning merry go round. The children at the Misty Hollow School stood around her singing, "Enna's in a pickle! Enna's in a pickle!" She was embarrassed and humiliated to once again be lying on the ground with no memory of how she got there.

On the walk home from school, Enna veered off the road and stood in the ditch as if she were looking through the fence. Charlie yelled at her, "Come on we've got chores to do before we can play!" Enna was non-responsive to Charlie's comment. She blankly stood against the fence for a moment before regaining consciousness. Puzzled by her own strange lostness, she turned from the fence and continued down the road, but never mentioned the anomalous occurrences.

Later that afternoon, she and Charlie were playing hopscotch in the dirt. "Okay Enna, it's your turn!" Charlie said as he noticed her staring into space. The episode lasted about five seconds and Charlie didn't think much of it until it happened again a while later. Charlie walked over and looked into her eyes. They stared blankly upward as if looking lazily into another dimension or some invisible, distant place. He left her there and ran to his mother. "Momma, Enna is looking up!" Charlie screamed. "What do you mean she's looking up?" Lizzie asked. He explained, "Sometimes Enna stops what she's doing and looks up. And she blinks her eyes." "Don't be silly Charlie! Go play!" Lizzie demanded.

That night as Enna was eating supper, she dropped her fork into the plate, startling every-one at the table and causing them to notice her frozen in a distant trance. Her head and eyes turned slightly upwards with a blank stare, and her eyes were slowly blinking. "Enna!" Lizzie sharply addressed her, but Enna didn't re-spond; until finally she snapped out of it and no-ticed the peas scattered on the table in front of her.

Recognizing what Charlie described earlier, Lizzie spoke softly, "Enna? Baby? You feel al-right?" Lizzie reached over and checked her forehead for a fever. Her temperature felt normal. Enna replied, "Yes momma. I feel fine." Charlie blurted, "That's what I was telling you about momma! That's what she was doing this after-noon!" Albert Said, "Charlie eat your supper!" Lizzie asked Enna, "Do you know what you were doing?" Enna Said, "No Ma'am." Lizzie explained, "Honey you were staring into space. Do you remember doing that?" Enna Said, "No Ma'am."

Lizzie and Albert's confused and frightened eyes met in unison across the table as Lizzie continued to question Enna, "Are you aware that you were absent for a moment?" Enna responded, "I am not aware it is happening, until I wake up in trouble." Lizzie asked, "How long has this been going on?" Enna answered, "It started this week at school."

The next day, Albert and Lizzie brought Enna to see the doctor. He looked into her ears, eyes and throat while asking, "How old are you now Enna?"
Enna replied, "Eight." He checked her finger nails and her reflexes, then he asked her another question, "Have you had any problems since your concussion, like dizziness, fainting, eyesight or coordination?" Enna replied again, "No sir." He asked her to take short, deep, quick breaths, inhaling and exhaling in succession until he told her to stop. The doctor demonstrated how he wanted her to breath. Enna mimicked

the doctor and within a short time she began to hyperventilate causing an overpowering sensation of suffocation. The condition frightened Enna and caused Lizzie and Albert to become so distressed they leapt to her, but the doctor held them back gesturing that they wait. Suddenly, Enna's terror stricken hyperventilation ceased and she drifted into non-cognizance as if absent from her own existence. Her slow blinking eyes peered sleepily into the space before her. After several seconds, the episode ended and Enna sprang forward into her mother's arms.

The doctor turned to her parents and said, "That is a petit mal seizure. A type of Epilepsy. Although the sickness has been around much longer than any of us, not much is known about it. No one knows the cause. It could be head trauma, like the kind she suffered a while back or it could be hereditary. But since neither of you have a history of it in your families, I would lean more towards her previous head trauma being the culprit.

The seizures may be stress related or they could be brought on by bright light. I don't know the initial cause; however, the seizure we witnessed today was brought on by stress. Some people outgrow epilepsy. While others get worse. Enna's could eventually become full grand mal seizures, which are the convulsive type. We'll have to wait and hope for the best.

There are drugs to treat this, although they are not a hundred percent effective; but, they could lessen the seizures. Also, a new drug has been developed called phenytoin that many doctors are prescribing instead of phenobarbital, which carries more side effects. I think we will try the phenytoin for starters, and if that doesn't help, then we will reevaluate her case and try again."

The engine hummed monotonously along the highway. Enna sadly remembered how the kids at school laughed at her for all the stupid things that she had done this week. She reflected back to when the teacher called on her to stand before the class and recite the first five presidents of the United States. She had no sooner said, "George Wash...," that a seizure gripped hold of her. By the time she came to herself again, the whole class was laughing and pointing fingers at her. She also remembered when she fell out of the swing and landed on her head...and that humiliating song: "Enna's in a pickle, Enna's in a pickle, Enna's in a pickle." She wished that she could crawl back under the rock that her mother found her under and never come out.

The truck finally came to a halt in front of their house. Enna's self-loathing thoughts were interrupted as her mother stated the obvious, "Well, we're home." Then she added, "Who wants lunch? Bananas are finally available again so I bought a bunch. How does a peanut butter and banana sandwich sound?" Enna had never seen such a thing because of the war, but she was open to the idea.

Bananas on a sandwich became a southern favorite ever since their arrival for the first time in the port of New Orleans. Miss Rhody introduced Lizzie to the delicacy when she was a little girl, and it became her favorite sandwich.

Enna's reaction to the new cuisine was difficult to interpret. She ate all of her sandwich, but instead of making any comment, one way or the other, she just sat quietly staring out the window for a moment. Finally, she asked, "Momma, do I have to go to school this afternoon?" Her mother sweetly answered, "I don't think it will hurt for you to miss one afternoon of school. Why don't you go lie down for a while and rest. You can get a fresh new start in the morning."

Lizzie wanted to be upbeat and positive around Enna. She didn't want her to feel discouraged about her condition. When someone is sick, they deserve to be shown a certain level of compassion until they get well. Enna was normal in every way. She had no fever or pain. Her only affliction was when the seizures came to her like some mysterious phantom, and momentarily stole her consciousness away, withholding it from her for some strange unknown purpose.

There were so many things that Enna could not do by herself any more. She could not draw water from the well, for fear that she might fall in. She could not walk to school alone, for fear that she might step out in front of an oncoming vehicle. She could not cook, for fear of burning the house down around her. She could not hold a baby, for fear that she may drop it. There seemed to be a thousand opportunities for danger. Although the medication would help, there was no guarantee that a seizure wouldn't happen at the most inopportune time. The doctor's words played over and over in Lizzie's mind, "There is no cure. They could become convulsive."

If she didn't outgrow this illness, Enna's entire life would be defined by it. Every decision would revolve around it. Her choices would be made in consideration of it. Her friends, her spouse, whether or not to have children, her entire future would be determined by it.

The next day Lizzie walked the path to the school yard from the main road. It was a short-cut through the woods that led directly to the playground. She wanted to see how the children at school interacted with Enna during a seizure. She didn't know if Enna would be ostracized or mistreated. After all, children can be cruel. The convivial noise of children romping and playing could be faintly heard through the woods. She thought how beautiful the sound was as she drew near the edge of the playground, out of sight.

There was Enna jumping rope. The two girls holding either end of the rope, swung it, as they sang: "Enna and Johnny sitting in a tree; K-I-S-S-I-N-G; first comes love; then comes marriage; then comes Enna with a baby carriage." Lizzie quietly chuckled at the silly song. She remembered singing it when she was a girl.

All of a sudden, in mid jump, Enna went into a seizure and literally crumpled into a heap on the hard ground. Lizzie lurched as if she would run to her, but caught herself, hoping that Enna wasn't hurt. She came there to observe Enna's treatment by the other children, so she reluctantly waited and watched. No one bent down to help. They only stared. It seemed like an eternity. Her pitiful, sweet child lay in the dirt. The

children gathered around her, not saying anything; but, they wickedly anticipated her return
to consciousness, just so they could sing in unison, "Enna's in a pickle, Enna's in a pickle,
Enna's in a pickle!"
Soon, Enna came to. Due to her embarrassment
and rejection, she gathered herself into a sitting
ball, with her knees drawn to her chest by her
little arms. Tears trickled down her sad little face,
as the children continued singing, "Enna's in a
pickle, Enna's in a pickle."

Lizzie spread the bushes apart in front of her
and was about to step out of the woods, when
Charlie came bounding across the playground to
his sisters defense. He bent down, wiped the
tears from her eyes, and asked if she was okay.
She affirmed that everything was okay, so Charlie lifted Enna to her feet.

Then Charlie faced the crowd of children who
sang the noxious song and carelessly taunted
his sister. He told them, "The next person I see
picking on my sister, no matter how big you are,
will have to deal with me!" Charlie wasn't the
oldest or biggest kid at school, but he was big
enough and gritty enough to back up his threat.
No one ever challenged him on it either.

Being reassured by what she witnessed,
Lizzie turned and parted the bushes in front of

her as she made her way home. She was proud of Charlie and knew that he was there for Enna today, but there was no way to fully protect her from life's hardships without putting her in a box. Regrettably, she will have to learn to cope with each situation as it arises.

Lizzie felt ashamed for giving Enna a silly name that could be used by other children for cruelty. What could she have been thinking?

Enna's diagnosis caused the gears to start turning in Albert's mind. He had to do more to take care of her and all of his family. What would become of Enna? How could he protect her from herself? She needed constant observation. The house and everything around it posed a threat to her safety. There should be a porch rail to prevent her from walking off the edge. The open well in the breezeway posed the most danger. She can't be allowed to draw water or go near the well. Open access to a sixty foot shaft is dangerous to anyone and should be eliminated altogether. If they had electricity, he could install an electric pump.

The Rural Electric Association had announced plans to bring electricity to Misty Hollow. Some of his neighbors had prematurely installed wiring in eager anticipation.

Lizzie deserved to have modern conveniences like a washing machine. She had been drawing water and scrubbing clothes in a wash tub all of her life. They could even add plumbing for an indoor bathroom. But, the expense was more than he could afford. Their small farm did not provide enough income to support their growing needs. All the money that Lizzie had saved while he was overseas was long gone, and they had tightened their belts to the last notch.

Just last week, he was offered a job as a foreman with the county road crew. He knew how to build roads and bridges as well as operate heavy equipment. These skills were picked up as a young man while working for a construction company out of Missouri. That job kept him away from home all week and away from his wife; but, the county job would allow him to be home every night with his family.

There were things to consider like the crops and the milking. However, Charlie was old enough to help out with the plowing, and Lizzie was already doing the morning milking. The other work around the farm could be done in his spare time. Therefore, Albert made the decision to accept the job offered to him. He determined to have that well closed in less than a month.

Chapter 18

The elusive whip-poor-will sang its vexatious spiel in the tall standing pine tree above Miss Rhody's house. Roy's dilapidated body sat slumped in the wheelchair on the far end of the porch where Rhody left him to get some fresh air. The whip-poor-will had worn out its welcome, but there was nothing he could do about it.

Introspection of his previous, hedonistic lifestyle occupied Roy's time, no matter whether he was awake or asleep. The stroke had reduced him to nothing more than a troubled mind, full of bad memories, held captive by a feeble, dysfunctional body. Though he could see and hear, he had no voice to speak, or physical dexterity to make gestures of any kind. He was totally reliant upon his sister, whom he still considered to be a religious nut.

Roy's memories of his drunken father haunted him. His old man had spent every day and most nights spewing hatred toward them. There had been constant threats of murder or physical harm. Many times they had to flee into the woods until he passed out, and it was safe to return home. Sometimes they slept in the woods, too fearful to go home.

Roy's guts were always full of hunger pangs. His back was always covered with rags. His feet cracked and bled because sometimes he had no shoes. His mother and sister were in the same condition. Their home was a tattered, dilapidated shack loaned to them by a cattleman who once used it to store hay, until he built a new barn.

If not for the Georges, who owned the Oil Mill above the Yazoo River, his family would have starved to death. After Roy's mother started doing their laundry and household duties, the Georges allowed them to move into a small but comfortable tenant house on the river, just below the Oil Mill. The Georges were offended by her ragged clothes, so they provided her with substantial clothing. She also brought home hand me downs from the George's children for Roy and his sister. Food and other necessities, like shoes, began to show up on their doorstep.

His father's evil nature swelled out of resentment toward Roy's mother because she was doing what he never did- provide a living for the family.

Late one night, Roy's father came home drunk and set fire to the house, while they slept. If not for the night watchman at the Oil Mill, they would have surely perished. He saw the bright glow down near the river and realized that one of the tenant houses was on fire. His report stated that when he arrived at the house, Mr. Hoots was standing guard with a shotgun. The night watchman tackled him, and they fought in the river for control of the weapon which was lost during the scuffle. Hoots did everything he could to prevent the rescue of his family from the fire.

The sheriff arrested him and charged him with three counts of attempted murder and destroying private property. The jury was out for five minutes before returning with a verdict of guilty on all counts. The judge sternly sentenced him to sixty years of hard labor. His family walked out of the courtroom satisfied with the verdict and the sentence. They were relieved to be shed of him.

His father's sixty year sentence came to an abrupt end after serving twenty years of hard labor, not because he was released by the state, but because he was murdered. The prison cafeteria floor ran red with his blood when an angry inmate slit his throat for taking a piece of bread from his plate.

After the fire, Roy's family was penniless, naked, and hungry. The Georges; however, out of the goodness of their hearts, saw fit to help by purchasing a small farm for them with a modest dwelling. Sixteen and malnourished, Roy worked the farm along with his mother and sister.

At that time, Rhody was courting their neighbor, Stanley Fletcher: a man of industry and resource. It was Stanley's idea to combine their farmland, use his hired labor to work it, and share the profits. The plan allowed his mother to resume her work for the Georges and for Roy to get a job at the Oil Mill. Stanley was a shrewd, but honest business man, even from a young age. He also had an eye for Rhody. He kept her close by working her as his personal secretary for his multiple businesses.

By the time Roy was nineteen, he acquired itchy feet and wanted to roam. He learned the way of the cowboy on a large ranch in Texas while also becoming a happy drunk. He was not violent like his father, but he was reckless and hedonistic.

On the day of his mother's funeral, Roy was drunk and belligerently insulted the pastor during the eulogy. He called him a "Bible thumping fool, peddling false hope to the weak and gullible." That pastor was his own cousin, Hilliard Hoots. However, Hilly never acknowledged Roy's comment. He lovingly continued to tell everyone about the day Mrs. Hoots was saved and her greatest prayer was that God would somehow get her son's attention before it was too late.

The bothersome whip-poor-will flew deep into The Hardwoods, where it could barely be heard. Roy welcomed the peace and quiet until he heard footsteps and saw the faint glow of a lantern coming in his direction. Rhody sat down in the chair next to him while holding the lantern up near his squinting face. She asked, "How are you making it Roy? Are the mosquitos eating you alive yet?"

She made idle conversation because she knew that he could not answer her. His only capable response was to raise his eyebrow, roll his one good eye, or grunt. So Roy did all three as she continued to hold the blinding lantern too close to his face. She had been his caregiver for over a year now, but had seen no improvement in his condition since the stroke.

Rhody extinguished the lantern with a lite puff of breath so the mosquitoes would not be attracted to them. From the dark she asked, "Roy, do you remember that time Cousin Hilly came to our house down on the river? Daddy was drunk as usual and was about to beat momma for wearing that new dress that Mrs. George had given her. You and I were scrawny teenagers who couldn't stand up against daddy, but Hilly was a big, strong young man with his own family. He caught daddy's arm by surprise just as he was about to strike momma. Boy...the look on daddy's face when he turned around to see that big ole boy holding his arm and shaking his head side to side. Hilly smiled and told him, "Unk, you gonna have to settle down! God don't like folks beating his children!" Daddy's face turned three shades of red. He was so mad he could eat nails. There wasn't anything he could do to stop Hilly because he was so strong and so big. Hilly led him by the arm over to the corner of the room and sat him down in the floor like a schoolboy. That was the only time I ever saw daddy put in his place, until the Sheriff led him away in handcuffs. Do you remember what Hilly said to you and daddy that day?" Roy grunted, which most likely meant "no." Rhody continued, "He told both of you that life does not have to be this way. Christ came to give us life and to give it more abundantly. Both of you scoffed and stormed out of the house!" Roy's memory was jogged a little. He did remember what Hilly said, but he had no idea what he was talking about. He remembered thinking, "How could a tortured man hanging on a cross fix everyone else's life when he obviously couldn't fix his own life?"

Rhode pressed on, "Roy, you're seventy years old. Your health is not improving. You will not live forever. Don't you think its about time to ask Jesus to save you before it's too late?" Roy grunted loudly and bucked a little in his chair as a response. Obviously, her comments made him feel very uncomfortable. He wished that she would go away and leave him alone. What could Jesus save him from? A stroke? Being stuck in a wheelchair? Not being able to feed himself or bathe himself? A nagging sister?

Chapter 19

It had been two years since Albert hired out on the road crew. He and Lizzie were prospering. His job was going well. As road foreman, Albert acquired a work truck with gas, tires, and maintenance, provided at no cost to him. He was able to park his own personal truck which saved him the expense of maintaining it. With Charlie's help, they had bumper crops of corn and hay. Albert bought three more milk cows, doubling milk production. Lizzie and Enna kept them milked twice a day. Albert built a concrete vat with a faucet near the road and filled it with cool water from the well. The milk cans were stored in the vat, until the milk truck came by to get them. Albert also wired their house for electricity. Furthermore, he left no evidence of the well in the breezeway. Water was being pumped, on demand, directly into the brand new kitchen sink that he installed along with new kitchen cabinets. The convenience of the indoor bathroom made them feel like royalty. Lizzie especially adored her modern washing machine and refrigerator. With the newly installed rail, they no longer worried so much about Enna falling from the porch.

The doctor was unable to find a better medication for Enna; therefore, her seizures continued unabated. She spent her days talking to Max who was three years old and had grown into a big fluffy sheep. He wasn't allowed in the house anymore, but hung out with Elly Mae in the yard.

Anytime Enna walked out onto the porch, Max was aware of her presence and ran to her. He was sensitive to her needs somehow and when she was in danger, during seizures, Max leaned close to stabilize her. Everywhere Lizzie went, Max went with her; even to school, where he waited patiently outside the door until she returned to him. Max loved Enna, but had nothing to do with the other children, and Charlie made sure they did not taunt him in any way.

Mr. Roy perked up when he saw the trio coming down the road. Charlie riding Buck, with Elly Mae trotting along beside them. After tying the horse to a low branch so it could be pulled down easily to graze, he and Elly Mae headed for the porch.

Grandma Rhody walked through the door with a tray and three glasses of ice tea. She was watching for Charlie and anxiously anticipated his weekly visit which was very good for Roy's spirit. "How are you doing Charlie? Your momma an' nem doing okay?" Charlie responded, "Yes ma'am. They are fine." It was always the same greeting and the same response every week.

Elly Mae ran around the house with her nose to the ground as Charlie climbed the steps onto the porch and hugged Grandma Rhody. He then turned around and shook his old friend's hand while looking deep into his eyes searching for the man he once knew. Mr. Roy received his hand into his lap and gripped it with as much strength as he could muster, and Charlie said, "Mr. Roy, I believe you are finally improving some!" The corner of Mr. Roy's mouth turned upward and he grunted a broken, "Uh...huh!" Encouraged by Roy's good spirits, Charlie continued, "I heard a new joke this week, you want to hear it?" One corner of Mr. Roy's crooked mouth turned slightly upwards and his eyes sparkled as he nodded his head in agreement. Charlie Said, "Okay!" And as he began telling the joke Grandma Rhody attentively leaned forward, already smiling in expectation of the punchline. "Well, one time there was this preacher who received an invitation to supper by a family who never came to his church. In fact, the last time he went over to speak with them they told him to leave and never come back! Because they had treated him so coldly in the past, he was very surprised by the invitation, but he thought, "Maybe this family has had a change of heart and wants to meet God." So he shows up for supper that evening and in the middle of the table was a platter heaped full of fried chicken. He told the family, "Great! My favorite food!" He quickly said the blessing and then tore into that chicken. By the time he looked up again he realized that he had eaten the whole platter of chicken all by himself, except for one piece. He was slightly embarrassed and apologized to the family, but they graciously smiled and said, "It's no problem, you eat all you want." So the preacher reached for the last piece and finished it off too.

Well, after supper, the preacher excused himself and stepped out onto the porch to stretch his legs. He was standing there sucking and picking his teeth when he noticed a little boy sitting on the porch with his feet dangling. The little boy had not been at the supper table so the preacher asked him, "Son, I didn't see you at supper tonight, weren't you hungry?" The little boy answered, "I don't like chicken." Then the preacher looked out across the yard and noticed there were chickens laying all over the place. Some were wheezing and some were not breathing at all. The preacher looked down at the boy and asked him, "What's wrong with them chickens, son?" The little boy exclaimed, 'I don't know preacher, but they're dying faster than momma can cook em!'"

If Mr. Roy had been able to slap his leg and bellow, he would have; but, all he was able to produce was a toothless, half grin with one slanted eye, while leaning back slightly in his chair. An occasional syllable hopped across his naked gums, as each one slowly escaped his weakened diaphragm, "Huh....huh....huh...."

Grandma Rhody shrieked with laughter while proclaiming, "I believe that's the funniest one yet Charlie!" With the punchline still hanging in the air, Grandma Rhody mirthfully said, "That preacher joke made me think about something that I had forgot to mention to you Roy. A while back, our cousin Hilly retired from his big church in Tupelo. My goodness. I guess it was about time. He has got to be at least eighty-three years old by now. But, from what I hear, his age hasn't slowed him down any. He and Fancy have moved into the old Stennis house. I hear that he has accepted the pastorate at our little church. I also heard that before he even unpacked his suitcase, he called a meeting at the church with every preacher, deacon and layperson in the area. Supposedly, he has been praying for revival to break out among his people in this community for sixty years. He wants to start a weekly day of prayer to be held right there in the church. He also wants to invite every faithful Christian in the county to participate."

Roy kind of snarled and grunted in absolute indifference to the idea. He still didn't care for Rhody's religion. As far as he was concerned, she could just keep all that to herself and leave him alone.

Chapter 20

The hogs squealed and fled in a consolidated herd, frightened by the pack of wild dogs. The vicious animals converged upon a young shoat that was strategically sorted from the herd by the calculating beasts. The alpha male clamped its knifelike fangs into the throat of the frantic pig, tearing into the jugular, releasing the blood and maintaining control while the remainder of the pack held various other extremities.

The loud ruckus awoke Albert from a sound sleep. Disoriented, he sat up on the side of the bed realizing that something was going on at the hog pen. He scrambled in the dark for his boots and shotgun, dropping a fistful of shells that rolled helter-skelter across the floor.

The noise of Albert's clumsiness, along with the commotion outside, awoke Lizzie who rose immediately and flipped the light switch to illu-minate the room. By then, Albert was leaving the house in his underwear and work boots car-rying a loaded shotgun.

Dawn was breaking through the trees as he bolted towards the hog pen. The hogs huddled fearfully in a far corner away from the dogs that were ripping the entrails from the pig and fighting among themselves for possession of the carcass.

Albert fired directly into the pack, killing one dog instantly, while the mass of lead pellets speckled their mangy hides with stinging pain. The rest of the pack scattered, grievously yelping in all directions, scaling the fence, and disappearing into the thick underbrush without a trace.

After dragging the dead animals from the pen, Albert buried the two carcasses together in the same hole. By then, he could smell breakfast cooking over the stench of the hog pen. He was content to leave the herd to their own care and returned to the house.

Coffee was brewing and Lizzie stood over a pan full of bacon and eggs. She informed him, as he tromped across the room with his heavy boots, "The biscuits are almost ready. You need to clean up, and please put some pants on." Without a word, Albert returned the shotgun to its prominent place above the mantle and obediently followed the commands of his bossy wife.

At breakfast, the conversation centered around the dogs. Albert observed, "During the depression, people couldn't feed their dogs so they had to fend for themselves. Many of them starved; but some, with survival instincts, found other dogs with the same instincts and formed packs. These packs were lead by a dominant dog who was the meanest and toughest. They are hungry and will kill anything or anyone. I've always heard about wild dogs, but that's the first ones I've ever seen."

Obviously distressed by the presence of wild dogs, Lizzie looked at Charlie and Enna, pointing her finger while saying, "You two stay near the house until we can decide if those dogs have moved on."

Albert reinforced the decision, but added, "Buddy, if you go anywhere outside, you take the shotgun and keep it close. Enna, you stay near your brother." He continued, "Better put all the livestock in the barn until this blows over, except Max. Tie a rope across the steps and let him hang out on the porch for Enna."

Confinement in the barn didn't bother the livestock since Charlie put a couple ears of corn in each trough. He also filled the hay racks and made sure their water troughs were full. Max was not accustomed to being dragged. He balked at Charlie's attempts. "Come on, Maximus. You're supposed to be on the porch." Charlie liked to call him Maximus because the name sounded heroic. Enna could hear Charlie wrestling with Max from inside the house and walked onto the porch. When Max saw her, he ran straight to her, leaving Charlie out in the yard with a bumfuzzled look on his sweaty face.

The less than romantic song of lovesick Cicadas quieted as their stridulations ended for the season. The sultry heat of summer began to change into the cooler climate of early autumn. As the fearful dread of wild dogs faded away, the livestock was turned out to graze the remaining green grass before the first heavy frost.

Charlie and Enna explored the path through the hollow leading to Grandma Rhody's house. The teacher at school assigned Charlie's class a project to gather insects before cold weather sent the bugs into hibernation. Charlie lagged behind, digging under a rotten log, while Enna and Max walked along the fern enveloped path ahead. Max veered from the path in search of edible vegetation, but not out of sight of Enna, who walked further up the trail to a clearing near the creek where she and Charlie sometimes swam.

The deep pool was hewn by swift water in a curve where it also cut into the bank causing a very large oak tree to lose its foundation and lean out over the pool. The large tree trunk created a natural platform over the pool where Charlie and Enna jumped into the water.

As she reached the clearing, Enna was startled by a mangy dog snarling at her in the edge of the ferns. Soon, more snarling dogs with chupacabra features surrounded her, leaving no way of escape. The beasts crept closer in a methodical stalking manner, positioning themselves to prevent her escape. Enna stood terror stricken and was unable to scream for help.

Max inconspicuously came from behind and touched her sweaty palm with his fuzzy muzzle. He purposefully and calmly walked past her into the center of the clearing, towards the leaning tree, drawing the dogs away from her. They pressed him against the steep bank overlooking the pool at the base of the tree. He walked onto the leaning tree trunk, and the dogs followed. As Max reached the fullest confines of the tree, the dogs lunged and pinned him between the sturdy branches. The furious attack sent light fluffs of wool floating in the air until they became too saturated with blood to float.

Finally, a horrific scream bellowed out of Enna as it had been trapped deep inside and was mysteriously released. Charlie's head tilted upward. His eyes looked intently in the direction from which he heard the scream. He jumped over the log, grabbed his shotgun, and bolted through the ferns. As he drew closer, he heard the dogs viciously attacking. It was his first thought that Enna was their victim, but Looking past her, he saw the dogs scrambling through the branches fiercely attacking Maximus and each other. Max's pure white fleece was now red with blood. The vicious dogs tore at him mercilessly until Maximus was dead. The mongrels gloried in their nefarious killing by emitting the sound of mean laughter much like a pack of hyenas. Charlie fired two shots, in succession, with his double barreled shotgun. With them, he killed all of the dogs, putting an end to the evil beasts once and for all.

Enna shuffled slowly onto the leaning tree, her mind muddled by the disturbing sight. Bracing herself against the stout branches, she sat on the trunk of the tree near Max and laid his bloody head in her lap. Disenchanted, she pulled Max's body from underneath the stinking dead dogs which were piled over him. Without emotion, she sat stone faced, holding the only real friend she ever knew.

Charlie placed his right arm under her blood soaked legs and the other across her back to lift her from under Max's bloody head and away from the scene. As he carried her down the path, she looked back at Max laying dead among the carcasses of his tormentors.

Grandma Rhody came quickly when she saw Charlie struggling up the hill with his sister in his arms. Having heard the two shots, and then seeing Enna soaked in blood, induced her to imagine the worst tragedy. But, all the years spent midwifing trained her to be calm in every quandary.

She pulled Enna from Charlie's arms and ran into the house where she placed her on the bed for closer examination. After searching and finding no wounds, she came out onto the porch and proceeded to examine Charlie as he sat in her favorite rocking chair. He was still breathing hard from the strenuous climb. Charlie interrupted her examination, and said, "The blood came from Max, Grandma. Wild dogs killed him at the swimming hole. It was a horrible sight. I've never seen Enna like this. I don't think she will ever get over it. She saw the whole thing, and she ain't said a word since it happened." Grandma Rhody asked, "What were the two shots that I heard?" Charlie described how it came to be that all of the dogs were on the tree at once and confined to a tight cluster making it possible to kill the whole pack with a double blast at close range. She nodded her head in understanding as he told the story. Then she solemnly told Charlie, "I am concerned for Enna. I'll stay here with her while you fetch your parents. Ask Lizzie to bring her a fresh change of clothes.

Grandma Rhody returned to the bedroom with a pan of warm water. After removing Enna's bloody clothes, she gently bathed and put her to bed where she sat holding her hand, humming a sweet melody to soothe the poor child's anguish.

Chapter 21

Weeks passed, but the memory of Max's brutal killing remained fresh on Enna's mind. Silence and grief persisted, causing everyone to be concerned. School work and chores were apathetically neglected. Vivid dreams woke her from fitful sleep every night.

Of all the people around her, Albert was the only one familiar with her condition. He had experienced severe symptoms of it himself after living through trauma befitting an adult. Gruesome images were permanently imprinted in his own memories. They still remained fresh and haunted him frequently. He was among the hordes of rushing soldiers on the beaches of Normandy who were faced with innumerable, German placed, land mines, which killed and maimed thousands of his fellow soldiers almost immediately upon landing. Many, who were fortunate enough to sidestep the land mines, were cut down by machine gunners protected by bunkers on the ridge above them. Albert was compelled to crawl over the dead bodies of his friends and fellow countrymen whose bodies were mangled and strewn about.

He witnessed the most horrific sight when a soulless soldier crawled past him on mangled forearms. The shock ridden man was oblivious to the fact that he was missing his lower body and dragging his entrails behind him.

On another occasion, in a different battle prior to Normandy, he was knocked down when an unseen heavy object blindsided him from across the battlefield. It threw him to the ground with such force that the wind was knocked out of him. As he lay frantically gasping for breath, the battle raged on. Finally, recovering from the heavy blow, he rolled over to his side seeking the heavy object that caused his downing. Adjacent to his own face was the face of a severed head. The face was one that he knew too well; it was cousin Eddy's face. He had observed Eddy advancing in front of an American tank, just a moment before.

Albert tried to block those images from his mind, but they were too deeply imbedded. He never shared the things he saw in battle with anyone.

As far as Albert knew, the only thing that could help Enna's condition was time. His mother always liked to give God credit. She said that the Lord could fix anything; but, the Lord didn't fix cousin Eddy, or the thousands of other Christians who died or were permanently mutilated in the war.

Grandma Rhody visited Enna daily hoping to see an improvement, but none came. She asked Lizzie and Albert to allow Enna to spend the weekend at her house, just to see if she could reach her. They agreed. Instead of driving, Grandma Rhody and Enna walked the short distance to her house, just before supper.

As they walked, Grandma Rhody cheerfully pointed Enna's attention to all of God's creation around her, such as the beautiful brown hues contrasted by the evergreen trees along the fence row. She showed Enna how the broom sage waved like a brown ocean as the wind swirled across its feathery tops. With an expression of awe and wonderment, she described the shape of a powerful stallion that she could see in the clouds, before it slowly drifted out of recognition. Without any acknowledgement, Enna shuffled along barely keeping up with Grandma Rhody.

When they arrived, Charlie waved from the porch, gleefully greeting them with his usual bad grammar, "Hey, about time y'all got here. Me and Mr. Roy are starving to death." Grandma Rhody had also invited Charlie to spend the night, hoping to make the atmosphere a little more cheerful for Enna. Supper was prepared ahead of time and was warming in the oven.

Enna's attitude remained stoic as Charlie forgot his purpose and began to focused his attention on the delicious food. Grandma Rhody was also preoccupied as she patiently spooned food into Roy's dribbling mouth. Enna moved the food around on her plate, but remained in her sad prison.

They eventually settled in the parlor where Grandma Rhody broke the silence. She said, "Enna, baby, you're gonna have to talk about what happened if you ever want to get past this thing. I am speaking from experience honey. Let me tell you a little story —A true story. Roy and I came up in an abusive home. Our daddy was an evil man. He had no love in his heart for any person. We endured regular beatings and watched our momma beaten bloody many times when she stepped between us and him. We had nothing but rags to wear. People looked down on us like we were the nastiest trash in the dump. Life was hard, but our poor momma had it the worst. She only wanted to take care of me and Roy the best she could considering the circumstances. I saw her give us food and go without when there was not enough to go around. When daddy beat her up, even breaking bones, she had no medical attention or medication. Sometimes she wouldn't be healed from one beating before she received another one. When our momma was thirty-eight years old, she looked like she was fifty-eight."

Enna's stone face softened when Grandma Rhody's sad expression revealed the pain in her own heart as she recalled the vivid details of her early life. Grandma Rhody continued, "There never was a day that we were not hungry cause daddy was a drunk and he was unable to hold a job. Any money that came into our house was spent on alcohol. His threats and terror increased over the years until one night after we were all asleep, daddy came home drunk and set the house on fire. The house was fully engulfed in flames when the night watchman at the cotton mill saw it and came running.

Daddy was standing outside holding a shotgun. The night watchman fought with him out into the Yazoo river where the shotgun was lost. The night watchman then rushed into the burning shack and rescued us. Thank God, we had no beds. If we had not been sleeping on the floor, we would have been overcome by smoke. We barely made it out before the whole house collapsed.

Daddy testified at his trial that he intended to kill his whole family that night. Anyone who came out alive would be shot. When I heard him say that as a sober man, it did something to me. I always thought the alcohol was the only reason my daddy acted the way he did. Until that day, I never fully realized that he had no love in him, especially for his own family.

I became sort of like you are today, too sad to live. I couldn't snap out of it. It controlled me completely. I awoke with horrible nightmares. I was sad to my core. I didn't want to talk about it, and I didn't want to come out of it cause I didn't have the strength or desire.

Then one day my cousin Hilley stopped by to see us. He heard about my depressed condition and wanted to help. He knew how things had been at our house. He even tried to talk to daddy about the Lord one time, but he showed no interest.

The relief of being delivered from my daddy's endless torment was short lived, and I retreated into myself. I was trapped in a prison of my own making; the prison of bitterness, resentment, and unforgiveness.

Hilley began to speak about all the evil things daddy did to us: pointing out every scar and talking about how mean he was. Hilly brought up things I had forgotten about. Before I knew it, we were having a conversation.

As I began to agree with Hilley about my reasons for hating my father and my unforgiveness towards him, Hilly reminded me how my new Heavenly Father was loving, gentle, kind, and gracious. He also forgave me for all the things I did against Him. I was absolutely floored when Hilly said that. He pointed out that God didn't have to forgive me, but He did anyway.

Hilley showed me the place in the Bible where God requires us to do the same for others. You see, Hilley had already led me into a personal relationship with my Heavenly Father, but I let the affairs of my horrible life take hold of me inside, and I lost sight of Him.

Enna blurted, "How did you get a new father?"
Grandma Rhody, surprised by Enna's sudden participation gently replied, "I asked God to be my Father." Enna studied on her response for a moment and then rebutted, "I already have a good father." Grandma Rhody confirmed, "You sure do honey, and he has been very worried about you,..but God is the Father of fathers. You can talk to Him anytime and He will listen. He wants to carry every burden you will ever have. You just have to give those burdens to Him. Are

you ready to talk about what happened to Max?"

Enna's expression became intense as she finally opened up to Grandma Rhody. She told how the wild dogs surrounded her, how they wanted to kill her, and how terrified she was. She wasn't able to scream for help or anything.

Enna's little face softened as she described how Max gently kissed her hand with his muzzle as if he were saying, "goodbye," and then walked out to face the wicked dogs. He drew their attention away from her and led them onto the diving tree. As he crept backwards, they crept forward, until they all stood together among the branches of the tree. There was no room for retreat. Max sacrificed himself to save her from the hungry dogs.

Grandma Rhody was astounded by what she heard and proclaimed to all of them, "That is similar to the story Hilly told to me when I asked God to be my Father." They all looked at each other in confusion, which prompted her to continue, "God so loved the world that He gave His only begotten son; that whosoever believes in Him should not perish, but have everlasting life." They still did not understand how this had anything to do with Max's death. It showed very clearly on their faces, but she was determined to explain. So, she said, "Let me start at the be-ginning. When God created us, He gave us a free will. That means, we are free to choose right or wrong. He gave us perfect boundaries to help us to distinguish the right from the wrong. But, we have always been prone to choose wrong rather than right. That is called sin. Because of His perfect nature, God always demands perfect justice, so He cannot allow sin. The punishment for sin is death. Since all have sinned; all are guilty. Like I said before, God loves the world and does not want to destroy us....Here is the best part.

God knows everything about His creation, even the number of hairs on every head. He knew before the world began that people would choose wrong. So, by His grace, He devised a plan to save us from His wrath.

He was born into this world as His own son. Jesus, through a virgin, lived a sinless life and then died in our place. He was buried. After three days, He was raised from the dead by his own great power; that same power one day will raise his children from the grave.

The Bible says that, "If you will confess with your mouth and believe in your heart, you will be saved." All we have to do is confess that we have broken His laws and need His forgiveness, repent of our sins, and ask Him to apply His sinless blood to our account by coming into our hearts and sealing us forever with His Holy Spirit. That Holy Spirit is God's person and power living within those who choose Jesus as their Savior, and He will remain there forever.

Do you remember hearing the name "Emmanuel" at Christmas? Emmanuel means "God with us." Through Jesus, who is Emmanuel, God will always be with His children, just as it was in the beginning at the Garden if Eden."

Grandma Rhody continued, "Enna, those dogs were going to kill you until Max expressed his perfect love towards you by dying in your place. That's what Jesus did; He died in our place. Max's story is similar to Jesus' story in other ways too: Max was a lamb; Jesus was called 'The Lamb.' Max was surrounded by dogs; Jesus was surrounded by men who were compared to dogs. Max died on a tree; Jesus died on a tree."

The more Grandma Rhody talked about Jesus, the more Enna's countenance improved. Even Charlie and Roy seemed to be intrigued by the story.

She continued, "Jesus is our hero. He came here for one reason: to die for us. However, you see, we still have a free will. God wants us to choose whether or not we want Him to pay our sin debt or not. Some people will make the wrong choice and reject what He did for them. That breaks God's heart, but He will not force us to make that choice against our will."

Enna exclaimed, "I choose Jesus!" And Charlie said, "Me too!"

Rhody looked at Roy who was spiritually uncomfortable. Although he had been watching and listening, he now looked away struggling inside between conviction and his own will to resist. Still looking directly at Roy she said, "Because we are sinners, we are literally forced to choose. No choice is still a choice; but, it is the wrong choice." Then she silently prayed that God would be gracious towards Roy and let him live long enough to make the right choice.

Chapter 22

The corners of Lizzie's mouth lifted into a smile when she saw Enna and Charlie strolling into the yard, side by side, excitedly conversing. She didn't know how Miss Rhody did it, but she was glad she did.

Not wanting to mention Enna's obvious return to normalcy, she said, "Well, it looks like you two enjoyed yourselves at Grandma Rhody's this weekend. What have y'all been doing?" Enna jubilantly responded, "We went to Church and met Grandma Rhody's Cousin Hilly. He is so nice. He talked with us about Jesus and he said that we are born again! It feels so wonderful momma! We feel so clean and fresh!"

Taken aback, Lizzie wasn't expecting an answer like that. She definitely saw a change in both of them. A glowing joy radiated from their faces, unlike anything she had ever seen before. She sent her children away for the weekend, and they returned to her as two completely different people. They seemed to be more mature somehow, like they possessed some powerful inner knowledge. What did Enna mean, born again?

In the middle of their conversation, Lizzie had rushed out to meet them and gave them both a

big hug while saying, "I missed you both so badly. Come into the house and you can tell us all
about it."

Albert heard them all excitedly talking from
inside the house. Enna's exuberant participation
in the conversation caught his attention. He
rushed out to greet them, falling into the middle
of the hug that was already in progress while
proclaiming, "Y'all look so happy and that
makes me happy." Enna brightly responded,
"Daddy, I love you! I'm sorry I had you worried,
but everything is okay now! Jesus saved me!"

Albert dropped to one knee in front of his
lovely daughter and hugged her again. He had
no idea what she was talking about, but her
glowing joy was undeniable. In all of his experience, he never saw any soldier saved from his
ghosts, but it looked like Enna was. He responded gleefully to her remark, "I don't care
who saved you, I'm just glad you're better. Let's
go inside where it's warm."

Once inside, they sat around the parlor talking about their experience at Grandma Rhody's
house and then at church. Neither parent understood what had taken place inside their children's hearts over the weekend. Although Albert
and Lizzie were both raised to believe in God,
He was never anything more than a passing top-

ic of conversation. Almost like he was not actually real, just someone you better believe in, or else.

The next day after Albert had gone to work and the children were gone to school, Lizzie walked to Miss Rhody's house for a visit. To Roy's chagrin, Miss Rhody was merrily singing a church hymn that had stuck in her head from church the previous day. Lizzie knocked on the door and yelled over the loud singing as she let herself in, "Anybody home?" Miss Rhody met Lizzie's pleasant smile with one of her own as she entered the parlor, "Hello Sweetie, Come on in." She nodded her head in Roy's direction and said, "Roy and I were enjoying some good church music." Roy rolled his eyes and grunted. Lizzie was entertained by their sibling brouhaha.

"Now, Mr. Roy, there's no telling how far you would have to travel to hear a concert like that." Then she laughed. But Roy only rolled his eyes and grunted once more.

Miss Rhody laughed at the facetious joke and at Roy's response. Then she asked Lizzie, "Wasn't it wonderful to have Enna talking again?" Lizzie responded, "Talking? More like chattering. That girl wouldn't let Buddy get a word in edgewise. I guess she had a lot bottled up, cause she talked full tilt until bedtime. Miss

Rhody, what did you do to my children?" Miss Rhody responded, "It wasn't what I did. It was what God did. Once they heard the Gospel, there was no way to hold them back. The Bible says, "We must become as little children in order to enter the kingdom of God." Roy and I saw that faith exhibited right here in this parlor Saturday night. I am so thrilled that God allowed me to see that. Nothing means more to me than to see my loved ones saved!"

Lizzie nervously agreed, but deep down inside, she knew her own soul was lost. Although she didn't know how to be saved, she was too embarrassed to ask Miss Rhody for help. Even though curiosity about her children's conversion had led her to Miss Rhody.

Chapter 23

The curious southern wind oscillated sporadically across the school yard. Red wasp fluttered near the eves and occasionally were trapped in the sunshine of the window panes inside the school. The unpredictable winter weather caused wardrobe confusion among the inhabitants of Misty Hollow. On one day, a coat was needed; three days later, there was no need for shoes or sleeves.

It was the day before the winter solstice, so the sun beamed from an odd angle in the sky. Because the winter solstice marked the first day of winter, everyone fully expected to be back in their coats the next day. However, as winter arrived, it was a nice day. The weather was warm, fair, and breezy.

Lizzie's momma always said, "A fair day in winter was a mother of a storm." She found that to be true. Ever since Enna's birth, she had become more attentive to the ways of the weather. The almanac rested on the kitchen table and was the most worn book in the house.

The winter time's warm southern breezes, made Lizzie restless, knowing that a collision of cold air and hot air was the recipe for severe weather. She hoped a storm wasn't brewing, but an ominous sense of dread welled up inside of her very similar to the fear she had on the day Enna was born.

Enna sat within the shadow of a large barren oak tree, out of reach from the burning sun that occasionally blared from behind the swiftly moving clouds. She giggled to herself as she thought about the times Max crawled up into her lap, not realizing that he was no longer a wee little lamb but had grown into a full sized sheep.

Enna and Max had spent every recess alone watching the children play and socialize with one another, but never with Enna. Being ostracized by the normal children was something that Enna had come to accept, but it didn't stop her from being sad and lonely. She observed friendly interaction between the girls her age and wondered what it would be like to have a best friend with which she could share all of her inner most thoughts, dreams, and secrets. She wondered what it was like to have sleepovers, birthday parties, and do girly things with other girls while being accepted and included.

It was just a few days before that Enna had talked to Preacher Hilly about how the other children laughed and made fun of her; how they never included her or wanted to be her friend. He lovingly told Enna that those girls most likely weren't interested in being true friends to each other much less anyone else; that Jesus was the only real friend any of us have. He proved His love to us by dying for us when we were still his enemy. Now that is a true friend that none of us deserve.

A tingling sensation, similar to goosebumps, flooded over her. She felt God's presence inside of her, giving her unmistakable confirmation to the truth spoken by the preacher. She felt His assurance that she would never be lonely again.

The sound of a clanging bell jolted Enna from the sweet fellowship taking place between her and her Maker. Recess was over, and it was time to go inside.

Class was far underway. The students were silent as they focused on the assignment given by the teacher. A loud clap of thunder startled them from their fixation. An instant, blinding streak of lighting flashed and struck the bell tower causing a single ding from the bell fol-lowed by a long rumbling of thunder. The tall windows usually provided abundant illumination, but they were darkened by the thick, black clouds and they rattled for what seemed like an eternity through every long rumble of thunder. The trees began to whip and twist casting away any remaining leaves or dead branches. Some tree tops were violently wrung free and rolled away.

Frantic teachers urgently herded their students into the hallway by pushing and pointing, unable to speak above the screams which were nearly drowned out by the intense howling of the wind. Immediately, as the classrooms were evacuated and the students were packed into the hallway, the roof peeled from the school and floated away like a leaf in the wind. The colossus storm was alive with deadly power as a dragon pouring out its fury on the little schoolhouse. There wasn't a soul present expecting to survive the fusillade as the west side classrooms were turned into a million splinters that darted with such speed that they pierced the walls and were injected painlessly into the students flesh. The west side row of windows became shards of knifelike razors spinning and slicing. The wind pushed the west wall of the hallway against the east wall, which stood miraculously, creating a tight shelter and protecting the students from flying debris. Shortly, the howling wind subsided and was followed by torrential rain.

As the students were entering the hallway, Charlie had prayed that God would cover them with His mighty hand; just as he sat on the floor, he was rolled onto his side by the wall as it was pushed into place, protecting the entire student body and administration. Students screamed and cried from fear, but they were safe from the fiercest part of the tornado. After the storm passed, several of the older boys managed to push the wall over, releasing the trapped students, but exposing them to the heavy rain.

Other than a few bruises, Charlie was unharmed. No one else appeared to be injured badly either, except some had a few cuts and splinters. He observed the wall that covered them and remembered how the wind held it in position like a shield. Grandma Rhody said God was like a mother hen protecting her chicks under her wing and that image came to his mind. He was sure that God's hand was holding the wall over them, since the boys who pushed it away used hardly any effort. He knew the wind could have ripped it off easily, sucking them all out and tossing them across the landscape. Silently, he praised God and thanked him for protecting them.

Looking through the cold rain, Charlie searched for Enna, hoping she too was unharmed. On the other end of the hall, he noticed a commotion. Squeezing between the students that were circled, Charlie was shocked to find Enna flouncing uncontrollably on the floor, her eyes rolled back and slobber foamed from her clinched jaws. Suddenly, her back arched severely, holding the extreme position until she turned blue and began to gurgle for breath. Intense convulsions caused her body to draw into stiffness, so acute, that it produced spastic trembling.

Charlie pushed his way into the circle and took hold of his sister. Her muscles were tight and hard, even statue like, until instantly she fell limp and silent. Charlie used his shirt to wipe the slobber and rain from her face. He talked to her, but she was unable to respond.

Abruptly, as Charlie held Enna in his lap, her eyes rolled back in her head. Her jaws clinched tighter and her back arched much more severely than the previous time. Her blue face contorted with tortured tightness as deep gurgling arose from her restricted lungs and windpipes. The powerful convulsion grabbed her from the inside out; it held her there mercilessly until the vessels in her heart exploded causing every muscle in her body to relax and fall limp. She discharged one long final breath from her lungs as her spirit departed from her body —she was dead.

The circle continued to widened until every student and teacher were present. They witnessed Enna's tragic death and Charlie's grief as he wailed and gently rocked back and forth holding his dead sister in his arms. The cold rain continued to drench them all down to their souls. However, they continued to stand in the cold rain, mourning for Enna and ruminating over what they had just seen. They were overtaken by remorse and regret. Extreme sadness permeated the atmosphere. But none felt more remorse than Charlie because he was the one who commanded Enna to get into the wagon. The doctor suggested that her injury could lead to convulsions and they did

Chapter 24

The winter Solstice would have passed almost unnoticed if not for the death of Enna Pickle. Christmas being four days away caused deep grief for her family. The Christmas tree, strung with new fangled electric lights and loaded with gifts, sat lonely and dark in the corner; just as the Pickles sat lonely and dark around the parlor, each deeply involved in their own individual reflections of Enna. Each gently sobbed intermittently as precious memories crossed their minds and touched their hearts.

A reverent knock at the door disturbed the quiet rumination. They each looked toward the door, but none moved. Shortly, Hilly Hoots opened the door and peered inside at the heart-broken family sitting in the dark room. After seeing who was there, Charlie rose to greet him.

"Come in Brother Hilly. Sorry for not answering the door. We're just not ourselves after what happened to Enna."

Although they acknowledged his presence with a nod, Albert and Lizzie continued their silent grieving. Hilly broke the silence with condolences to the family, but they only produced a strained smile and nodded again. They could not respond with words because they had none.

Although death had stolen their first daughter: Marie, they had no explanation for it, or ability to comprehend it's purpose.

Finally a question was angrily blurted from Lizzie who sat stone faced with ankles crossed and her hands folded in her lap, "Why does God hate us?" Hilly respectfully responded, "God doesn't hate you Lizzie. God loves you." Lizzie shakily continued, "If He loves us so much, then why does He keep taking our children?" Hilly walked over and sat on the sofa next to her. He reached for her folded hands in an effort to comfort her. She angrily snatched them away from him and demanded, "Answer me! You are supposed to be a man of God, then answer for your God! What kind of God kills innocent children and throws their lives away?"

Hilly moved back in his seat ever so slightly and patiently answered her question. "God has been working since the very beginning to salvage mankind from the destruction brought into this world by man through sin. God keeps every child safely under his care, He never throws them away. The enemy is the one who steals, kills and destroys. God is not the enemy. I know that you have heard about Job who lost all ten of his children in a storm. That storm was created by the enemy for the purpose of killing

Job's children. In addition to losing his children, Job also lost his fortune. Well, to make a long story short, God gave Job back double everything he lost except his children. Do you know why?" Intrigued by the story, Lizzie asked, "Why?" Hilly answered, "Because Job's children weren't lost to him; they were all safe in God's care. They were waiting in heaven to be reunited with their parents and siblings. Job's family was still intact. God saw to that.

Rhody told me about Marie's death and about your miscarriage. But, let me encourage you. Enna is safely in God's care. So is Marie. So is your nameless baby that was miscarried. And so is Charlie. Your family is intact. God has seen to that.

Just a few weeks ago Enna and Charlie both chose to accept Jesus as their Lord and Savior. Through Jesus, they are accepted by God into His family. The same family to which your other two children already belong, due to their innocence. God has done His part in keeping your family intact, but you have to do your part too! You and Albert should turn your lives over to God by accepting Jesus as your Savior. Then you will be reborn spiritually and able to receive God's forgiveness for your sins and you will be accepted into God's family. It would be a shame for all your children to be in heaven and you choose not to go."

Albert had been silently listening from across the room. He stood and walked over to Lizzie, kneeling before her with a hand on each of her knees, he cried in contrition and confessed to her, "Hilly is right. My momma told me those same things. I always ignored them because my daddy did. But now I see where he was wrong. I don't want to be wrong. I want to keep my family forever. Lizzie let's s do what Hilly says."

Under strong conviction, she and Albert fully surrendered their will. Hilly prayed with them to receive the free gift of eternal life that can only be offered through Jesus, the Lamb that was slain from the foundation of the world.

Chapter 25

The stench of putrid, rotten eggs burning into Roy's nostrils was nauseating. He bent over with his hands on both knees attempting to vomit, but his stomach was empty producing only dry heaves. The odor was so bad, he feared his stomach would turn inside out. Roy opened his eyes to a weighty darkness penetrating into his very soul.... Where was he? What is this place?.... Visibility was near zero.

Roy squinted, rubbing his dry, burning eyes with the index fingers of both clinched fists. Poisonous, yellow smoke suspended around him in a motionless fog. Burning, yellow sulphur produced intense, dark blue flames and suffocating fumes. The sulphur burned hot enough to melt into a blood-red lava which pooled around his submerged feet. He ground his teeth in pain from the furnace like heat produced by the blue fire and molten blood-red sulphur.

Surprised to find himself naked, he searched his body and lifted his feet from the molten lava, expecting to find them burned. But there was no damage and his flesh was dry and cracked. The pain coursed throughout his entire body, which was void of any water. His tongue craved moisture from any source, but there was none available, or would there ever be.

A sea of wailing and crying and gnashing of teeth could be heard, although visually hidden by the darkness and fog. Somehow, he knew there was never any darker sound of sadness any place on earth—not even during the times of the black plague or all wars combined.

A naked figure stood in his presence, wailing and crying. Roy peered closer through the fog to see his father's face within inches of his own. Surprised, he stumbled backwards in shock. The fog separated and his father was fully revealed. His throat was slit and worms poured from the open wound. The expression on his face was sad, but sincere. This was the only other time that Roy had ever seen him sober and alert, since his trial. He drifted into Roy's space and opened his worm infested mouth to speak: "I hoped I would not see you here." Roy confusingly asked, "Where are we?" His father's scratchy voice emanated, carrying the stench of rotten flesh, "We are in hell! — We are surrounded by the fearful, and unbelieving, and the abominable, and murderers, and whoremongers, and sorcerers, and idolators, and liars. The smoke of our torment will ascend up for ever and ever giving testimony to our hatred for God and our unforgiven sins."

Roy didn't want to believe what he was hearing. He wasn't a bad person. Even though he had done some bad things in his life, he had also done some good things. The good should have out weighed the bad! Roy emotionally responded, "I don't belong here! I'm not evil like you! God wouldn't send me here!"

His father's scratchy voice expounded on the truth that he had been taught by his own father when he was a little boy. He rejected it then, but it was all very clear to him now; and he repeated it to illuminate Roy's understanding, "This place was created for Satan and his followers. We are not sent here by God....We choose to come here as Satan's followers....We could have chosen to be God's followers, but we rejected the only door available into His Kingdom; that door is Jesus!"

Roy, remembered how Enna and Charlie indisputably proclaimed their faith in Jesus. He then nervously and anxiously responded, "I believe in Jesus!" His father laughed indignantly and rebutted, "Of course you do!....Everybody in hell believes!....The problem is, we should have believed before we were condemned forever!....Every knee will bow and every tongue will confess that Jesus is Lord....of things in heaven, of things on earth, and things under the earth!"

Roy was distraught as his dire condition became apparent. He realized that he was in a real place of everlasting destruction, where torment is heaped on top of torment, where people are unaware of day or night, where the fire is not quenched, and the worms eating his flesh would never die! He dreaded that it was a place where he would eternally hear the sea of screams from people forever suffering with their own remorse and regrets, playing them over and over in their minds like a broken record. He too was remembering the choice he should have made and didn't!

But wait! Something his father said brought a small glimmer of hope, a blemish in his story. Perhaps he was wrong. Perhaps his being here was a mistake! "You said hell was created for Satan and his followers; if that's true, then where is Satan?" His Father pointed up and said, "He is not here yet! He is gathering lost souls! He roams to and fro upon the earth; seeking whom he may devour!"

As his father spoke, the yellow fog slowly moved past them and they found themselves standing on the precipice of a bottomless pit.

Visibility across the empty space was perfectly clear. It was a great gulf separating two worlds: the place of torment in which he and his father were standing; and the paradise of blessing, filled with people who were held in the bosom of love and care.

Though the distance was very great across the abyss, Roy could very clearly see his mother on the other side. She was so beautiful and healthy. Joy emanated from her and she shimmered with light. She was no longer dirty or dressed in rags. Instead, she was cleaner than any clean and wearing a pure white robe. Stanley Fletcher was also there and he appeared the same way. When Roy saw her, he felt deep shame and regret. He wanted to go to her and tell her how much he loved and missed her. Looking in every direction, he asked his father, "Is there a bridge we can cross?" His father answered, "There is no bridge. No one is able to cross the great gulf. They cannot come here, and we cannot go there." His father continued, "Though we cannot go there, we will leave here at some point. God has determined a judgement against His enemies. When the time is full and the last righteous soul is gathered into heaven, the end will come and we will come before Him! There will be no earth or sky, only God sitting on a great white throne with masses of people gathered from the beginning of time, both small and great! There will be young, sweet mothers who selflessly cared for their husbands, fathers who worked hard to provide for their families, and children. There will be great men who served their communities with pride, teachers who sacrificed their whole lives for their students, derelicts who wandered alone and never bothered anyone. Also, there will be sweet, little old grandmothers and patient grandfathers. Many of the people there will be good people. Hell is full of good people! My daddy used to tell me that people are not saved by works of righteousness. They are only saved by grace, through faith in Jesus.

God has books and books of information on all of us. Our whole life has been recorded and on the day of judgment, those books will be scoured for the one reason God should let us into heaven. All of our works, no matter how good they may have been, are just filthy rags to Him.

Finally, He will open the book of life. Anyone who accepted Jesus as their Lord and Savior will be recorded in that book! If your name isn't there, you will be cast into the lake of fire, which is the second and final death. That will be your final fate because you denied God's grace that was extended to you out of great love. You will be doomed to endure everlasting torment."

When hearing all that his father said, Roy somehow knew that it was true. The truth that was rejected by his heart while on earth was now mysteriously and clearly confirmed in his mind.

Roy longingly stared across the abyss at his mother and his brother-in-law, who appeared to be so happy. Although darkness prevailed on his side of the abyss, everything and everyone on the other side of the abyss were illuminated by a magnificent glow. The Great Light was not like the sun, which scorched the earth; but rather it permeated the atmosphere and everyone there joyously shined and were filled with vibrancy.

Suddenly One appeared out of the Great Light. He was clothed in pure white down to His feet, and wearing a golden vest and crown. His head and hairs were white like wool, as white as snow. His eyes were as a flame of fire. He spoke directly to Roy with a voice of thunder, "Roy! Roy! Why do you choose death over life?"

Roy fell to his knees into the molten, blood-red sulphur which spilled over the edge of the abyss. The intensity of his irrelevant scream was ignored by those around him who were suffering the same fate. He leaned out over the abyss, reaching and screaming for Jesus to save him from hell. But Jesus did not reach for him. Losing his balance, he fell into the abyss. His only desire was for the one he had already rejected. As he was falling into the bottomless pit, he screamed the name, "Jesus," "Jesus," "Jesus!!!"

A loud crash shook the house, startling Rhody from a deep sleep. Rising from her bed, she stood in the darkness struggling for cognizance and quietly listening in an effort to identify the sound that woke her. A muffled shuffling sound was coming from Roy's room. Upon entering, she found Roy helplessly floundering on the floor, wailing and crying. He had fallen out of bed and was working tirelessly with his limited abilities to raise himself from the floor. Miss Rhody took hold of her distraught brother to comfort him, but he would not be consoled. Profusely, he cried and attempted to speak into the darkness past Rhody. His adamant behavior caused her to look behind her, but nothing was there. His semi-paralyzed tongue spoke one distorted word over and over, hysterically and broken, "He...sus!" "He...sus!" "He...sus!" "He...sus!" "He...sus!"

Chapter 26

The procession of mourners sadly filed past the open casket. The line extended from the front of the church, out the front door, and all the way to the barren oak trees where people gathered in one large assemblage, waiting to weave into the line, like yarn being pulled from a basket. It didn't seem to matter that it was Christmas Day. Strangely, no one rushed home to their decorations or other Christmastide trappings. Instead, they all felt the loss of the Pickle family and were thankful to God that none of their own children were killed in the tornado.

While living, Enna could make no friends. However, her tragic death being witnessed by every child in the four room school, made them all her friends by affiliation. Although they were somewhat familiar with death, it had never been validated until death actually claimed Enna's life before their very eyes. A melancholy spirit spread throughout the entire group forming a bond of camaraderie that is so common among youth.

Albert and Lizzie originally planned a small ceremony for close family members inside Miss Rhody's church. Lizzie's three brothers and their families were present for the first time since they left Misty Hollow so many years before. Also in attendance was her Uncle Edward and Aunt Earline who brought their daughter Cathlien and her family.

The plans for a small ceremony had to be revised after the very large crowd of mourners continued to linger in the church yard, desiring to be present for the funeral, even though there was not room in the old plank church. It was decided that the funeral would be held at the graveside in order to accommodate the large crowd.

The mourners standing at the back door of the church parted, making room for the pall bearers as they brought Enna's casket down the steps. They carried her body up the hill, placing it over the newly dug grave where the esteemed Reverend Hilliard Hoots stood on the mound of dirt freshly excavated from the cold winter sod.

The old preacher sang *Amazing Grace* as the hillside, filled with mourners, wailed from grief. His voice echoed down the prominent hill and bounced off the back wall of the church. Being in his early eighties, he was no longer the physical specimen that he once was; however, what he lacked in physical appearance, he made up for in oratory presentation. His scrawny, slumped shoulders caused his black frock coat to appear too large. But his strong voice clearly resounded across any space, reaching it's target like a well placed arrow.

The old preacher finished his lovely song, then gazed across the sea of mourners with his open hands raised in front of him as a signal for everyone to whimper softly, but pay attention. As the crowd grew quiet, he slowly, but forcefully proclaimed, "1 Corinthians 1:27 says, "God— has chosen—the foolish things— of this world— to confound— the wise!" He then paused for a moment allowing the statement to hang in the air by itself, giving everyone the opportunity to digest each word. Then he continued, "God has confounded the "so called wise" since the beginning of time!— One perfect example of that is when he sent a five hundred year old man to build a giant ship on dry land. While building it, he preached to the people about their sin and described rain, which at that time did not exist. And due to that rain, along with all the water from under the ground, the whole earth would some day be flooded above the highest mountains. Now, that sounds like a foolish thing, even today! But I know for a fact, that right here in the highest hills of Mississippi, there are beds of extinct oyster shells. Furthermore, the creeks are full of sharks teeth, along with other fossil remains belonging to sea creatures. Scientific evidence points to a world-wide flood!

The people did not believe it then; and some don't believe it now! The "worldly wise" of Noah's day said it was not possible! But God confounded them and their faithless, dead bodies floated in the endless ocean until they decomposed and sank to be buried in the mud beneath.

Another perfect example of "God choosing the foolish things of this world to confound the wise" was when He sent Moses to free the Hebrew people from Pharaoh's grip. God didn't come against Pharaoh with a big army!— No!— He sent a fugitive murderer to inform him that grasshoppers, lice, flies and frogs were going to make him release the Hebrew slaves. —How foolish is that? God sent ten separate plagues against Pharaoh, but the mighty ruler did not believe a single one until it was too late! People are no different today! They still scoff at God's Word!"

Pharaoh considered himself to be the wisest of all who walked on the earth! He even proclaimed himself to be a god! People today still think they are wiser than God! That's why He uses foolish things to make fools out of prideful and arrogant men! The Bible says, "The foolishness of God is wiser than men!"

Today is Christmas. Some of us mark this day to celebrate the birth of Jesus, the promised Savior and King of the world! His arrival into this world is the prime example of how "God chose the foolish things of this world to confound the wise."

First of all, His mother was a virgin! She had never known a man and yet, she gave birth to the Son of God! Second of all, she gave birth to the King of the world in a filthy animal shelter! Thirdly, she laid Him in a dung filled animal trough for a cradle! Fourthly, angels announced his birth to lowly shepherds and not to the dignitaries of the day!

Later, Jesus as a twelve year old boy, stood in the temple with the religious elite of his day and confounded them to their faces! Those so called wise and knowledgeable men of God piously sat in the presence of the Most Holy One and never suspected that He was God!

Later, when Jesus was grown and performed miracles, the people believed that He was the promised Savior. But they were not looking for someone to deliver them out of sin, they were looking for a Savior to break the yoke of Rome off their necks. What did Jesus do? He once again "chose the foolish things of this world to confound the wise!" Did He ride into Jerusalem on a massive white stallion? —No! He rode into Jerusalem riding a puny little colt of a donkey!

Did He choose generals and powerful politicians to surround himself? —No! He chose foolish people like John the Baptist who dressed like a caveman and ate bugs! Were His disciples the educated and religious elite? —No! They were ignorant fishermen, hated tax collectors, and harlots! The people who believed and followed Him never won a popularity contest! —No! They were the blind, the lame, the leprous, the adulterous, the scandalous, the rejected of society, sinners unable to stand on their own merits, but forgiven by the grace of God! —As were some of you! Some of you know the Lord! You were one of those "foolish things" that He chose to confound the wise! Christ died for the ungodly and He chose the foolishness of preaching to reveal Himself to a lost and dying world!

Little Enna Marie Pickle was one of those things God chose to confound the wise! She was forced to be a loner by her peers because she was sick! She was like those we read about in God's Word who were healed by the Master!

Enna was a born again Christian! My cousin Rhody Fletcher led her straight to the Lord shortly before she died! And just like those sick ones in the Bible, the Master healed her. But you might say, "Preacher, God didn't heal Enna, she still had seizures and it was her sickness that killed her! She is dead!"

I heard the same reports that you heard. But I did not believe it then and I do not believe it now. Jesus said in John 11:25 and 26, "I am the resurrection and the life, he that believes in Me though he were dead, yet shall he live. And whosoever lives and believes in Me will never die." Do you believe this? That's why I say that I don't believe that Enna is dead! God promised me that she cannot die! — "Whosoever lives and believes in Me will never die!" I ask you now! Do you believe this?!"

Reverend Hoots pointed a bony index finger at the crowd in front of him as he asked them again, "Do you believe this?"

Holy conviction pierced every heart and the crowd began to fall prostrate to the ground in a wave, beginning at the top of the hill and descending to the very bottom as God's mighty hand of grace brushed across them. Even Roy left his wheelchair and fell on his face in the presence of God's holy power. No one could move nor did they want to. There wasn't a nonbeliever among them.

Preacher Hoots also lay prostrate alongside his wife, Fancy, and the many faithful Christians who had been praying for revival in the community for several months. There was nothing else to say. No more preaching needed to be done. The prayer that he and Fancy had prayed for sixty years was finally being answered. God had done exceeding, abundantly above all that he could ever ask or think! The Holy Spirit shined like a torch through Hilliard's simple sermon, dispelling the darkness and bringing revival to Misty Hollow.

Enna's torch also burned bright from the hilltop where her dead body lay in the simple pine box, suspended over the grave that was dug next to her sister Marie. And it continued to burn bright even after she was lowered into the ground and covered with dirt.

Though she and her sister are with the Lord, their bodies await the resurrection where they will be transformed with new glorified bodies as Jesus calls for them to "Come forth!"

Chapter 27

The regeneration of every soul present at Enna's funeral was not the only great miracle of the day. Roy Hoots rose up from the ground a whole man, able to stand without assistance and able to speak clearly. The stroke no longer held his body in a state of contortion. He walked down the hill that day pushing his own wheelchair. His heart was filled with praise and thanksgiving to the Lord who gave him the supernatural dream of hell which caused him to finally see that he was a sinner in need of repentance. The power of God's Word, spoken through Rhody's preaching, caused him to believe and make a sincere confession of faith. Jesus saved him and in the days since the dream, his newly acquired faith led him to spend hours beseeching God for the miracle of healing.

On the edge of the cemetery, stood a giant antebellum magnolia. Its waxy evergreen leaves hung densely to the ground creating a facade sufficient enough to conceal Mrs. Stokes from the crowd. She stood in the midst of the low hanging limbs, ashamed of the cuts and bruises which adorned her fragile body.

As the preacher spoke of the "foolish things" and those who were the "rejected of society," she looked down at herself. A lifetime of poverty and bad choices had left her malnourished and abused. She was wearing the best clothes in her possession which were nothing more than rags. She didn't understand why God would want something as worthless as herself, but she desperately asked God one simple question, "Lord, am I worth saving?"

Then suddenly, she felt a strange, warm, love, flood over her and through her. An overpowering desire for God made her knees buckle and she fell to her face in the moist, black dirt covered with one hundred years worth of decaying magnolia leaves. From that moment, she knew God had saved her. It didn't matter anymore what her husband did to her; she was free.

Mrs. Stokes came home that day a new person. The malaise of fear that Mr. Stokes held over her vanished. His attempts of fear mongering continued and became even more severe. Nevertheless, she displayed the greatest defiance in the face of it all by openly forgiving him for beating her, causing him to recognize his loss of intimidating power that once made her tremble at his presence.

After seeing the change in his wife, he secretly followed her to Misty Hollow Church where the revival continued unabated. The church was filled, shoulder to shoulder, with new converts and the curious who had heard the stories about God breaking out at Misty Hollow.

She made her way to the front, where Roy Hoots was standing next to the empty wheelchair in which God held him captive two years. He told how his sister never gave up in prayer for his salvation. He testified how his own body became a prison forcing his trapped mind to relive his entire miserable life remembering all the evil past deeds he had committed against God and family. He shared about his vision of Hell and how God miraculously convinced him of his lostness. Finally, he stressed to them about his ceaseless prayers for healing and the experience of being healed by the Lover of his soul.

Roy was determined to know nothing but Jesus Christ and Him crucified. That internal knowledge was enough for him to stand boldly before the enormous crowd and proclaim his love for the One who saved him and set him free.

As Mr. Stokes stood in the doorway, straining to look past the hordes of people, he spotted his wife standing against the wall. Her attention was placed solely on the man speaking near the podium. It was his drinking partner, Roy Hoots, preaching to the crowd about someone named Jesus. Strangely, he noticed that his friend Roy possessed the same magnificent nature his wife came home with a few days prior. As Roy was praising this Jesus and giving Him glory for the healing of his body and the saving of his soul, the Spirit of God moved. Conviction fell over the unrepentant souls in the congregation. Mr. Stokes was one of them. He began to cry and forced his way to the front of the church, seeking relief for his troubled soul. Hilliard Hoots stood near the alter to receive those coming forward. Then he knelt and invited every person in the group to kneel also. He asked them to pray after him this prayer, "Father, I have felt the conviction of your Holy Spirit and I realize that I am a sinner. With your help, I repent of my sins and place my faith in Jesus who died to pay for my sins. I be-lieve that Jesus died, was buried, and three days later, the Holy Spirit raised Him from the dead. This is the same Holy Spirit that brought me to the alter and the same Holy Spirit that will one day raise my body from the dead. Amen."

The Stokes' lives were forever changed by their encounters with Jesus. Mr. Stokes no longer drank or abused his wife. In time, their old natures became unrecognizable as they were transformed into new people.

They both acquired jobs and attended church weekly. Eventually, when their economy improved, they left the broken down shack on the north ridge. They moved to the town of Natchez where they built a prosperous horse and carriage business. Northern tourists were intrigued by the beautiful old couple, who lovingly shared their testimonies with everyone they met.

After thirty years of hard work, the business prospered and everything they owned was placed in a trust. The profits from it funded a Christian orphanage in Natchez, founded by them, called *Chariots of God Children's Home.*

Uncle Thomas and Aunt Emily became strong supporters of the bulging Misty Hollow church. They were instrumental in leading the newly formed missions committee into not only sending new converts to seminary, but also in planting new churches in the surrounding communities. Also, they worked tirelessly to get a new modern school built to replace the one destroyed by the tornado. The community wanted to honor them by naming the school after them, but they humbly refused. They insisted that the new school be named in memory of Enna Marie Pickle, whose death at the school affected every life in the little village.

Uncle Edward and Aunt Earline, along with Lizzie's brothers, returned to Eutaw, Alabama filled with the Holy Spirit and sparked a revival there also. Edward and Earline reached out to families that had lost sons in the war, while Lizzie's brothers became evangelists who held tent revivals in remote areas of the country.

Phineas and Penelope Bartholomew brought their healthy little girl, Arabella, to Enna's funeral to show their last respects. Little did they know that their lives would be changed forever. Arabella, now eight years old, stood between her parents holding each of their hands as the spirit of God moved that fateful day. Being raised in an Orthodox Jewish home, she had never heard that Jesus was the Savior of the world. But as God's hand swept across the hillside, her supernaturally tight grip on her parents could not be released by them. Her own collapse to the ground pulled them to their knees. Quickly they realized that it was God's grip on their hands and they were overtaken by God's grip on their hearts as well. For the Bartholomew family, there was no denying that Jesus was indeed the Messiah. Before that day, Penelope had no be-lief one way or the other. But Phineas was taught that Jesus belonged to the gentiles, which had nothing to do with Jewish beliefs.

They became the first of many messianic Jews in the county, but at the cost of all their friends and family. One day, however, Arabella came home from school with a small group of her own Jewish friends. She had secretly con-verted them to Messianic beliefs. Apparently, she was holding a Bible study during lunch break. Being much loved by her friends, they decided to listen rather than ostracize her. Those children eventually won the hearts of their parents for "Yeshua" and a new messianic syna-gogue was erected where those families wor-shipped.

Hilliard and Fancy Hoots retired from the pastorate and returned to her mother's and father's old family cabin on the banks of McIntyre Scatters.

Over the years, an unusual migration of coyotes moved into the Delta and thinned the skunk population, making Jacinto's cabin livable once more. McIntyre Scatters remained a wilderness. There, Fancy renewed her love for everything wild.

They also took in three half-grown boys left orphaned when their parents were taken under and never again seen by a flood on the Yalobusha River. Because the boys had no food, no family, and no place to go, they were beholden to Hilliard and Fancy. They worked hard to make a home for themselves while tending to the needs of the aging couple.

Although Fancy and Hilliard were in their eighties, they were able to give the boys a good home life, seeing them grown and married. Hilliard supported the boys by preaching revivals, where all three came to know the Lord.

The boys were accepted as part of the family by Hilliard's and Fancy's grown children, who lived and were surrounded by their own families, in Tupelo.

When Hilliard and Fancy passed away from a fever, the whole family met on the banks of McIntyre Scatters. There, they buried them next to Jacinto and Rebecca LeBreax, inside the rusty wrought iron fence of the family cemetery.

A beautiful magnolia was planted by Fancy at the time of her father's passing. It grew to be very large and fully adorned with Spanish moss. In later years, a thunderstorm damaged the tree, giving it a permanent bow. The tired, old tree now slumps over the graves like a guardian; its moss gently sways back and forth in the breeze as if languishing in grief over the precious saints buried beneath its roots.

Albert and Lizzie were forced to enlarge their home as new additions to their family arrived. Lizzie gave birth to three babies within the next four years. First was a daughter who they proudly named "Victoria." Next came "Nicholas" who was named after Albert's grandfather. Last came "Winnie Estelle" named after the two matriarchs of the family.

The children came as a blessing to Albert and Lizzie, adding to the blessing of their three children in heaven. It is said that God is the same yesterday, today and forever. And just as He gave Job ten more children, He gave Albert and Lizzie their three.

A day didn't pass that they were not gathered around the kitchen table listening to Albert as he read from the Bible. Lizzie and Albert were determined to lead them in the way that they should go, so when they were old, they would not depart from it.

Albert built a small cabin off of the back porch for Grandma Rhody who came to live with them. She was a precious soul to the entire family. Charlie's younger siblings were the last three children delivered by her and she was determined to help raise them. In her lifetime, she'd gone from Rhody: the drunk's daughter, to Miss Rhody: the business man's wife, to momma: the surrogate mother of Lizzie, and finally to Grandma Rhody: the beloved grandmother of seven grandchildren. Their home became a refuge for traveling missionaries passing through Misty Hollow. Every time one came to speak at her church, Grandma Rhody invited them to stay at their house. The powerful influence of those missionaries inspired Charlie and his younger siblings. They loved to hear the stories of far away places and how Jesus was able to change the lives of primitive and backward people, no matter their culture.

By the time Charlie was 18 years old, he was a lovable big brother to his three younger siblings. They looked up to him, placing him on a pedestal that grew taller and taller in his absence, after he was drafted into the military.

Prior to America's official entry into the Vietnam War, President Eisenhower sent US soldiers in to help relocate 450,000 Vietnamese from the north to South Vietnam. Charlie was one of those soldiers. He even volunteered to serve another full tour of active duty, which kept him away from home for a total of four years.

By the time he returned home, he was a very mature and well traveled, 22 year old man. His younger siblings thought of him as some sort of celebrity and were always under foot. However, he was eventually able to get away to himself long enough to see the old home place where he and Enna grew up.

Charlie propped his foot upon the bumper of Stanley Fletcher's old truck still parked where Grandma Rhody left it the day she stopped driving. He looked down the long front porch of the old, log house and across the sagging barbed wire fence into the empty pasture. His mother and father no longer milked cows or kept hogs. The hen house no longer housed chickens, but instead was converted into a garden shed. The patina of a rusty tin roof was all that was visible of the barn built by his great grandfather, where his ancestors worked, but he and Enna played. Sweet gum saplings now surrounded the rotting structure. Pokeweed and pigweed congested the entrance of the hallway once trampled by livestock.

The path leading to the spring was over grown with weeds due to the availability of modern inventions like well pumps and cars. There was no need to carry water or walk the shortcuts through the woods anymore. Most of the old shacks that once dotted the ridges above the hollow were abandoned as the occupants passed away. Their progeny left them in the cemetery, seldom returning to pay respects. Their old, rusty farm implements were soon hidden by a growth of bushes and trees. Educated children rejected the hard life lived by their parents and were enticed away by the opportunities offered by the modern world outside of Misty Hollow.

Charlie reminisced about the times he had ridden Buck down the path to the spring with Elly Mae trotting along behind him. Those two were the best companions a boy could ever have and he still missed them. Although he was a grown man, he cried when his momma's letter came with the sad report that Elly Mae crawled under the house and died. It happened just after Albert came home with the news that Buck was found dead in the back pasture.

Charlie removed his foot from the bumper and walked through the gate of the old fence. He proceeded down the weedy path that led to *The Hardwoods*. He stood at the eternal spring, still bubbling from its source deep under the hill and spilling over the moss impregnated cypress box his father had built so many years before.

The old foot path was no longer the poor man's road. It had once again become dominated by bobcats and deer traveling along the creek in search of food.

Wading through the ferns, Charlie searched along the rocky hillside just above the old path. There it was; the place where Enna was born. The rock shelter looked small in comparison to what he remembered so long ago. He could see himself as a little boy peering through the limbs of the fallen treetop and his momma holding a wet baby in her arms. In his thoughts he could still hear Enna screaming at the top of her lungs with ear splitting intensity. It was almost as great as the sirens he heard in Vietnam.

Though he was four years older than Enna, it seemed as if his own life began on the day of her birth because his earliest significant memory was the day of the first tornado when he and Grandma Rhody went to search for his momma in the hollow. A smile spread across his face when he thought about all the happy times that he and his sister shared together. If Enna had lived, she would be 17 years old and he was sure they would be the best of friends.

The amiable thought turned to lament and then to pity for poor Enna when he remembered the song. That sad, sad song that followed Enna all the way to the end of her short life. The lingering voices of children from long ago rang in his ears, still taunting his precious little sister:
"Enna's in a pickle!"
"Enna's in a pickle!"
"Enna's in a pickle!"
Charlie stood blankly gazing into the birthplace of his dead sister; his mind locked into the mournful memories of the past. Painful, stabbing pricks pierced his heart. After all these years, he still grieved her passing, but he was

certain that he would some day see her again —
and she would be well — and they would continue to be the best of friends.

The End

And to God be the glory!

About the Author

Foolish Things: A Southern Tale by Carroll County, Mississippi resident William (Mark) Blaylock has been named by the Independent Book Publishing Professionals Group as one of the best indie books of 2020.

William Blaylock's book is a finalist of the Regional Fiction and Religious Fiction categories in the 2020 Next Generation Indie Book Awards, the world's largest book awards program for independent publishers and self-published authors.